Dear Anne,
This book was written
by my friends daughter
made me laugh out lo[ud]
Hope you enjoy it
With love
Becky
x

LIST LIFE

S Jackson

I have tried to recreate events, locales and conversations from my memories of them. In order to maintain their anonymity in some instances I have changed the names of individuals and places, I may have changed some identifying characteristics and details such as physical properties, occupations and places of residence.

ISBN: 979-8-6749-7304-1

Prologue

Ok, so the hustle and bustle of Christmas was over. Well apart from a few extended family get-togethers, where you have to pretend that you love turkey so much that you don't mind having it cold for the 5th time this week. Uncles ask you questions like … 'So, how's your job?'... I mean, this is a cop out question, it's like saying 'I literally have no idea what you do in your life but I assume you have a job.'

You know the days I mean, when you walk about asking people 'Is it Wednesday or Thursday?' The days where you have eaten your body weight in fancy cheese and crackers whilst watching back to back Christmas films. Well this is where we are right now. We are on what feels like the longest Sunday ever.

I'm lying in bed, freezing cold and have just started chapter three of 'Yes Man', which is actually a lot better than I thought it was going to be. It follows a year in Danny Wallace's life where he has to say 'Yes' to everything. A nice little stocking-filler from two years ago and I finally have gotten around to reading it.

My phone flashes with a text. I know that it's Brad because he has been rambling on to me for the past half an hour about the fact that he is struggling since his wife left him 18 months ago and last week the paperwork came through for the divorce, so it was final! It must be awful. I have never been married, I'm only 26, but I have been with Jack for eight years and I know that if he just decided to walk out now, apart from the heartache of him leaving, I'd have to recreate my whole life and start again. Actually, that does sound kinda tempting.

Jack and I met at university and now live in Essex in an apartment, just around the corner from his family. We live right next to the underground station and just a short walk away from the town with its glamorous nail bars, expensive pubs, sports cars and everything you can buy with young money. We are a couple of those high flyers. Successful and living the dream…

Ok, ok, so maybe we were just extremely lucky and landed ourselves a one-bed, council flat in a really nice area, but we do have a sports car, a bargain Jack picked up a few years ago and when I can afford it, I get my nails done in a fancy salon.

The message reads:

I fell asleep on the sofa again last night watching back to back films. I need to stop doing this. I just feel really crap and I have no food in the flat...

I'm not sure why people come to me looking for sympathy. I don't have time for this sort of thing. People often tell me I'm cold-hearted but I think that if you feel sad then do something that makes you happy. So, I started typing:

Sort yourself out boy. Get up, shake yourself off...

Ok that sounds like advice I shouldn't be giving and he'll probably get all moody. **Delete* *delete** ... start again:

Wake up! Shower! Then put some crazy bright shorts on, find some shades, a cold drink, a beach towel and lay down. Shades on and blast 'I'm a dreamer' by Amber as loud as you can.

This may sound ridiculous but I used to do this when I was stressed or felt a little home sick at Uni and it sorted everything out. I would pour myself a cold glass of Coca Cola (add a bit of vodka, depending on the time of day), lay in front of my bedroom window, on a bright pink and green towel and turn up the music. It would make me chill out, make me smile and sent a buzz down my spine.

Well it always worked for me. However, all I got back from Brad was a photo of him in a pair of bright blue shorts lying on a bed and a message saying:

Y*ep! Done! now what*?

Well that was it. That was meant to solve all his problems, he must have done it wrong.

I get up and get in the shower, feeling rather confused. I'll do the routine myself, see if it still works. I throw on a pair of leggings and a jumper because its freezing, I grab a towel and head to the living room. Pineapple juice is my choice of drink as a Pina Colada is probably not a great idea at this time in the morning. I lay in front of the window so that I can see the winter sun and pretend I'm on the beach.

This is amazing. I feel great! Jack on the other hand seems a bit annoyed, huffing and puffing when he has to step over me and my shades whilst he's trying to get ready. Although he doesn't join in, he never questions what I do and I kinda like that about him.

I text Brad back.

You must have done it wrong. I've just tried it and I feel amazing! But I don't get a reply back …miserable git.

I met Brad at work. He wasn't in on my first few days because he was working on site, but everyone kept telling me we would get on really well due to the fact that he liked travel and eating unusual food and so do I. When he finally showed up about a week later, he didn't speak much, especially not to me. He shared some inside jokes with the other guys but I didn't really get involved. Then, one day I was speaking to Tom (we will get to him later) about how I had just moved into my flat and really fancied some sausages but I only had a microwave because the oven we'd ordered hadn't turned up yet. Suddenly, Brad interrupted and said 'Why don't you get microwaveable sausages?'

'Sorry, what? Do they even exist?' I replied. I didn't think Tom was listening to me let alone anyone else.

'Yeah of course, I have them all the time when I get in from a late gig.'

He sent me a link to a supermarket selling them and we spent the rest of the afternoon discussing different sauces I could make to go with them. That night I found him on Facebook and sent him photos of the sausages along with the selection of disgusting sauces I had attempted to make myself. He didn't reply for ages but when he finally did, it turns out he did the same that night and to get to the point we have been pals ever since. So, they were right we did bond over our love of food.

Today's plans are: Jack and I are going pop into town to get a few more bits for the flat because we have no storage and there are beads everywhere from where I made jewellery and attempted to sell it at a Christmas bizarre. The reason I say 'attempted' is because I stood out in the freezing cold for six hours and only sold one pair BUT I now have 30 pairs of earrings that only I love…silver lining and all that!

Then, this afternoon, my pal, Graham is going to come round and we are going to book a trip to China. We were talking about China a few months ago and he said he had always wanted to go, so we decided to book a trip for early next year. You don't have to ask me twice to go on holiday.

Then, this evening, Natalie is bringing round a takeaway so that we can sit and watch *Bridget Jones* and eat our body-weight in pizza! Jack has decided to go to the pub with his pals...I don't blame him. It will be a very girly night. Well, plus Graham!

The shopping trip went well. We bought a cheap, tacky looking set of plastic drawers for my beads but who cares. It does the job.

While we were out, we stumbled across a black corner desk in a charity shop for £10, what a bargain! Not sure why we need a desk but it looks great and fits perfectly next to the sofa. It took ages to get the thing into my little fiesta so, I had to rearrange for Graham to come over a bit later.

Brad has been texting me throughout the day talking about how this year has been pretty good and how he wants to make sure 2017 is a great one. See, in the end the 'I'm a Dreamer' routine makes anyone's day; *you should try it some time.*

Anyway, Graham is here now and we are buzzing about China. I have known him since we were about 13 years-old, along with a few of my friends from school and they are all like family to me. Every year we would go away on the standard 18-30 holidays to Zante, Magaluf, Kavos etc. You know the list. We had the best times! There was always a big crowd of us on the way there and an even bigger crowd on the way back. But China didn't appeal to the others for some reason. I think it was a bit more expensive and a lot of them are saving to buy houses and cars.

Anyway, I grab us a couple of beers and we start looking at some tours on various websites. There are hundreds. You can do, food tours, history tours, work in panda enclosures and all the crazy adrenaline-filled weeks like rock climbing and bungie-jumping. After scrolling through loads of trips, we found one where you camp on the Great Wall of China, which sounds amazing! It also takes you into the rainforests and you get to eat in a place, famous for their duck pancakes. We both love the idea of that one, so I email the tour company and pop open a bottle of prosecco to celebrate.

Natalie is meant to be here in half an hour with pizza but with all this talk of China we make a call and ask her to stop at the Chinese takeaway instead. When she finally turns up with the food, Jack leaves for the pub and we all sit down and tuck in to our chow-mein and spring rolls.

Main topic of goss today is Natalie's new man. He sounds quite nice, but they all do at first. Then we don't see her for a while because she's so obsessed with him. Then she gets bored, they split up and we have another night of takeaway and films. She seems happy though, so this one might work out well.

Graham is talking to a guy he met online, but doesn't think it will go anywhere. He said he would rather be single for China – result! That means I can play match- maker when we are out there.

All in all, it was an amazing night!

Brad said he has been feeling great all day and is debating whether to stay at his parents and have a few drinks with them or go home and clean his flat…I know, it was a stupid question, so I decide not to answer and just ramble on about my evening.

But it turns out it wasn't a stupid question after all because he chose to stay and have a few drinks but has started being all mopey again. He said he has nothing to do tomorrow but needs to go home as he hasn't seen Mr Chow (his hamster) in two days and he will probably be starving! Oh bejeez.

Then I had an idea! So, I text him back…

I will write you a list of tasks to complete. You can complete them in whatever order you want and however you want, but they must be completed by the end of the day.

Chapter 1 – The First List

29th December

8.15

Do the 'I'm a dreamer' routine!

Make breakfast including a lime

Text someone a compliment between 11am-11.15am

Paint me a watercolour painting, small or big but you only have 15 minutes

Read a chapter of a book

Make plans for tonight

Find out a fact you didn't know about planes

Call your mum

Hug someone

Make dinner or buy dinner with chilli

Make a plan for 2017

……Send.

09.21

I haven't heard anything back for an hour now, maybe he has found something to do.

I should really get up but that only means moving from the bed to the sofa and probably dragging my duvet with me because it's so cold. I need to turn the heating on and it takes forever to warm up. It was never this cold when I lived with my parents and we lived in a 3-bed-house. I don't understand why heating is so expensive, surely it should be discounted in the winter because it a necessity.

Just as I am about to get out of bed, I hear my phone bleep.

I quickly grab it all excited that he has finally text back! The text displays two images:

Image 1: The bottom half of Brad's legs in another crazy pair of shorts and glass of orange juice. I'm assuming he is raving to I'm a dreamer and hasn't just severely messed up a selfie.

Image 2: Two tacos with scrambled egg, avocado, lime and onion… well that's what it said in the description. To be fair that looks and sounds amazing!

I chose a lime because 1) It's odd to have with breakfast so a bit of a challenge and 2) It's makes me think of that zing-kick you need in the morning.

Talking of breakfast, what am I going to eat?

I stroll into the front room dragging the duvet behind me and catch a glimpse of myself in the mirror. My messy ginger hair, black smudged make up round my eyes and rocking a pair of red fluffy socks. I point to myself in the mirror and wink 'Looking good babe'. I blow a kiss and strut to the kitchen, switch the heating on, open the fridge and sigh. We have a choice of natural yogurt and prunes or Muesli? No zing-kick in this fridge!

It's Christmas what am I thinking?! Grab a hand full of Celebrations and a mince pie and go back to bed because it too cold and Jack is watching some boring programme about the history of the railway.

Jack is a sports coach. He eats, sleeps, breathes football. He spends any other time in the pub with his mates or his brothers and his favourite food is curry. All of this I put down to the fact he is a stereo-typical 26-year-old lad. But then he watches stuff like railway documentaries or has a glass of wine whilst chilling to some old school jazz and I think maybe he is actually an 80-year-old man stuck in a young guys body.

I get back in bed and sit up against the cold wall. I start eating the chocolates and build a pile of bright coloured wrappers on the bedside table. After five minutes of scrolling through Facebook I receive a text from Brad.

Another Image: A book by Ben Elton called 'Post Mortem'

I'm not sure what it's about but there is a drawing of hang man and The Daily Mail describes the author as someone who '*provokes almost as much as he entertains'*. Well 'Post Mortem' means after death so although it looks like a good book, maybe he shouldn't be reading that if he's on his own and not feeling great.

Don't read things like that when you're feeling down. I quickly type.

Calm down Elise, someone might think you give a shit! Don't worry I'm fine it's a good book actually.

Ha! Funny boy, I don't give a shit actually, I'm 'ard!'

I've decided that reading is a good option so I will carry on reading 'Yes Man'. This is such a good book, saying yes to everything sounds like a great idea. I might try it. Starting from now!

I get up, get dressed, log on to my emails to see if the travel agent has emailed back with confirmation of our China trip.

You have 999+ unread messages. Jeeez, I should really start opening my messages. I click on the first one, it's from one of these online second-hand markets. The message reads:

Don't miss your opportunity to buy this Solid Oak dining table, seats 6!! Would you like to make a bid?

Erm 'YES!' I click on the link and scroll down.... WHAT!!!

Your bid must exceed £350.

Hmm well it has to be done. I just need to check my bank account first, to make sure I have enough.

Your balance is £42.

OK, so technically that's not even possible. Maybe I should leave my emails to another level of the game.

Jack gets out of the shower singing some football chant.

'Elise, what are you up to on 27th February?' He asks, while vigorously rubbing his hair with a towel. This is my chance to embrace my inner Yes man.

'Fancy going to see Spurs play Middlesbrough?'

Crap! No. No I don't.

Ok so maybe I'm not quite ready to be a Yes man. Maybe another day.

11.22

My phone buzzes and I quickly grab it.

It's a screen shot of a text to Evi: *Hi ya! Is there anything you need me to bring over? It seems like ages since we saw you last! Will be good to see you, Rikki and the kids. You have such a lovely family you should be very proud.*

I think Evi is the girl that lives in Holland Brad was telling me about. They are family friends and he and his family are going over there for New Year. Oh My God! I need to make plans for New Year! I wish I had pals in Holland or anywhere abroad for that matter.

Anyway, he is taking this list seriously, which is fun and the compliment is in the time slot.

I'm finally dressed and have ventured to the living room. It's so grey and windy outside and the rain looks ice cold. When we first moved in, I was so excited about having floor length, glass balcony doors with view of the high street and big green fields in the distance, but now I can't see a bloody thing with all this mist and it has been like that for the past month or so. I need to get out of here. I think Brad is now having a better day than me!

'Jack, if we go and get some brackets for the Chinese shrine/vanity stand thing, can you put it up this afternoon please?' I know! Wild, right?

'Sure! But there's a game on at five so let's go now,' he agrees.

I get ready and we head out.

15.45

Bracket shopping is so boring. This adult life isn't what I thought it would be. I thought moving out was meant to be exciting, turns out I was wrong. For example, have you ever chosen carpet? It's literally the most confusing thing in the world. You have hundreds of rolls of beige and grey carpet with all different price tags and you have to choose which one is the best beige. I mean, how often do you look at your carpet to know which one to buy?

Neither of us knew what brackets we were looking for and we had a row about whether a packet of nails was too expensive or not. Luckily, as per usual, a McDonalds saved the day and now we like each other again.

Changing the subject. Did you know American Airlines now

issue iPads instead of pilot flight manuals, which provides an estimated fuel saving to the airline of around $1.2 million per year? No neither did I, but it was the fact Brad found out about planes.

16.04

We are home and Jack is so eager to watch the game at five that he gets cracking straight away with putting the shrine/ vanity stand up.

I found it in a charity shop a week before Christmas. It's an amazing dark red wood vanity stand with oriental writing down each side and 2 small white lights. I asked the guy working behind the counter how much it was as I only had £20 on me. He said he thought it was more like £40 but the woman that owned the store had popped out for lunch so wouldn't know until later. I wasn't going to wait as I needed to pick my car up from the garage, so left it, went home and ranted about the whole scenario to Jack. Then on Christmas day, Jack surprised me with it, he said that he went back to get it and the woman had given it to him for £20! TYPICAL!

17.00

After all the drilling and hammering, I am finally chilling on my bed admiring my new feature. It looks beautiful. I'm just about to send a photo of it to Brad when he texts me first.

I open up the message and there is a photo of a painting.

Ok so before I explain the photo, I need to explain that I really would like a yacht. Obviously, this is a bit farfetched for someone on a mediocre wage and a million other things I could spend my money on. But ever since I told Brad that it was my dream, he has been convinced that one day I will actually own one.

Just before Christmas he sent me a photo of a different yacht every day from 1st December to 25th as a sort of advent calendar.

Anyway, so now you will understand why the painting he painted is of a small yacht with red sail on blue sea surrounded by a few birds, and down the side had 有一天很快.

Love it, what does it say? I reply.

It says 'One day soon'

Wow! Yes, this should happen. Ok, it may not be soon but I would like a yacht, even a small one. I love being on holiday and walking along the harbor, deciding which one I would choose if I was filthy rich.

Last year I was in Turkey and walked past a huge super yacht with 6 floors, an outdoor crazy golf course, indoor gym and luxury dining area out the back. I got a glimpse of the inside as the door was open and sitting there was a dark haired, extremely tanned gentlemen with a glass of whiskey, watching Who wants to be a millionaire! Is he taking the piss?!

Anyway, more importantly…

Have you made plans for tonight yet? I change the subject.

Kind of.... I thought I would kill three birds with one stone and call my Mum, ask her if I can go around tonight and then maybe she might hug me, sounds pretty sad but that counts, right?

Yes, that counts, although you need to have a longer conversation with her than 'can I come around tonight?'

Can I ask her if she can make me dinner with a chilli?

...No!

19.09

This flat is starting to depress me. It's so boring. There's no one around and it's always cold. The décor however, is amazing, if I do say so myself. We have based each room on different world themes so the living room is bright orange with Indian and Moroccan pictures, elephant ornaments and double curtains (Orange and Cream). The kitchen is based on a city theme and is very industrial, so, we have brick wall wallpaper and photos of cities we have visited. In the bedroom the bed has a huge, Chinese fan instead of a head board, my new oriental shrine and Japanese style bedding. The hall way is bright red with strange and unique bits on the walls, like football memorabilia and old school posters.

Then the bathroom is bright yellow and fresh, with a large canvas of a multi-coloured giraffe. Most people say it's too much but I don't care I love it. Colour makes me happy.

I think I will make some more jewellery. That also makes me happy!

I have set my little jewellery station up in the corner on my dining room table. Jack is watching Only Fools and Horses. The one where Rodney first meets Cassandra.

'Shall we order a takeaway tonight? Your choice.' He grins at me as if this is the most exciting thing in the world, and to be fair, he's kinda right. I love a takeaway! I skip to the kitchen to find the menus. We have loads stashed in a draw along with safety pins, elastic bands, carrier bags and playing cards. Everyone has a draw like that right?

I decide to have an Indian because I had Chinese the other night and curry is Jack's favourite. We order lamb dansak, chicken ceylon, rice, peshwari naan and saag paneer.

When it arrives, we chill out and watch Muppets Christmas Carol (his favourite Christmas film) followed by Love Actually (my favourite Christmas film). It's been an ok evening but I keep doing the same things, get up, eat, go shopping, eat, make jewellery, eat, watch a film. Brad told me earlier that he really enjoyed the list and that it was just what he needed. He didn't spend the night on his own, made someone smile with a compliment, painted me a picture, had a great time at his parents and said he was happy! Well at least I made someone else's day a good one. I need to get motivated myself.

Well tomorrow should be more fun. I'm going to see my Dad's family.

But for now, I am going to bed.

Good night x

Chapter 2 – What Happens in 2016 Stays in 2016

30th December

10.00

I'm very excited about today. I haven't seen my Dad's family in nearly a year and it's not as if they even live that far, just busy lives I suppose. Also, I have an excuse to wear the new top my parents bought me for Christmas, I love it! It's silk with a high collar and a red and green Chinese pattern. Very oriental.

I received a text from Brad this morning saying that he had the best day yesterday and is kind of sad that he doesn't have a list today. So I got all excited and am sitting here writing him another one but a little smaller as he said he did actually have to clean his flat and run a few errands.

Yesterday's list was to get him motivated and to make sure he wasn't on his own. Today's list doesn't need to be that deep so maybe just some fun things:

Eat an entire multi pack of crisps throughout the day

Wear red

Clean your teeth upside down

Tell someone you love them

Buy Mr Chow something nice

Buy yourself something nice

11.00

Right, I need to stop off in town before I get to my parents, I still haven't got a present for my secret Santa. I know it's late but I had so many presents to get before Christmas and thought I would save this one for the sales.

Every year my Mum writes everyones names on slips of paper and puts them in a hat. She then gets one of her colleagues at work to pick them out and send a text to each of us with the name of our secret Santa recipient, it's all very official. This year I got my sister's boyfriend, Hansel. His name is actually Craig but he met my sister in a pantomime where she played Gretel and he played Hansel and I just forgot his name, so I kept referring to him as Hansel and it stuck ever since. Hansel is an actor/singer/performer type guy, very confident and a bit of an extrovert. I think he drinks beer which is an easy present to get quickly, but maybe something with a twist to suit his flamboyant personality.

As we are walking around the shopping centre, I am trying to explain to Jack about the lists and how funny it was receiving a photo of Brad upside down cleaning his teeth this morning, with his mass of long curly hair hanging over the bed. He had a bright red face where the blood had rushed to his head, it was hilarious. Jack didn't seem too interested. He has been given my Dad as secret Santa so is trying to find a joke present but has a really serious face which is ironic and making me laugh.

'Oh Jack, wait! Can we just pop in here? They might have something for Hansel,' I shout after him because he is pacing ahead as if we are on an episode of Supermarket Sweep.

I have found this unique, little beer shop selling craft ale. I have always wanted to own my own beer shop, not selling craft ale but beers from round the world. How cool would that be?

I snap out of my day dream when I come across this chocolate flavoured beer! Ooo and salted caramel vodka. Boom! Sorted! Now to carry on the hunt for Dad's present.

16.00

We are finally at my parents and I dive upstairs, have a quick shower, put on my new Chinese top, ready for the family to turn up. The best bit of moving out is I am now technically a guest, so can eat all of the olives and peanuts put out for 'guests' but I also have the luxury of being able to jump in the shower and raid the wardrobes. My sister, Ava, has really expensive makeup and Mum shares the same taste in jewellery as me so I glam up, throw on a pair of oriental looking earrings I find in her jewellery box and finish the look with a splash of Daisy perfume. I just have to make sure they don't find out I have used their stuff.

Bouncing downstairs and feeling fresh. I grab a hand full of fancy-pants crisps and wander into the kitchen to see what food Mum has been making for tonight's shenanigans. Jack is in the living room with Dad watching the game. I can hear them shouting the same things they say every game 'Ahh, what a save!' and 'REF! Come on! How did he not see that?' I mean why do they bother? It makes them so annoyed and they always come away saying it was a waste of time.

As soon as I walk into the kitchen Mum turns round and whines.

'ELISE! I was going to wear those earrings today!' Crap! She noticed straight away. 'Listen, do me a favour and look after this curry while I go and get ready please. Everyone will be here soon. Just give it a stir now and again,' she requests, whilst stealing the earrings from me. Damn! Ok I will go and get some others later.

As soon as she leaves, I start stirring the chicken pretending to look like I am helping and scroll through Facebook. I am just watching a video, a girl from work posted, when Ava comes stomping into the kitchen.

'ELISE! Where's my eyeliner?!' She has her hands on her hips and her face is all screwed up. Oh good God, she's caught me too and I can't remember where I put it.

'I put it back in your makeup bag.' I lie.

'Are you pretending to look busy?' She changes the subject.

'No, I'm taking this job of sous chef very seriously actually' and I look back down at my phone.

'I dare you to put more chilli in there!' she laughs.

'Oh jeez, she will go mad!' But I accept the dare anyway, throwing chilli powder all over the dinner. I don't like too much spice myself but I know Mum's made a lasagne as well so I can eat that instead. I swig my wine and go and sit with the boys but as soon as I sit down, the doorbell rings so I leap up to see my Nan and Grandad at the door.

18.00

I love these people and all the cousins are quite similar, so we have a lot to talk about. Chloe is really grown up, she has a job with the Police and speaks very well. She always asks the text book questions like 'How's work? And how are things with you and Jack?' I'm rubbish with that kind of talk. My go to question is 'If you could eat anything at all, what would be your choice of a three-course meal?' Genius question! It makes people talk about food and finds out what kind of person they are. I judge people on their meal choice, for example, if they go for mango and chilli chicken skewers, Indonesian curry and a knickerbocker glory then I'm hooked but if they say 'I don't do starters, then maybe a roast but without gravy and finish with a crumble.' I move on. If you're interested, mine is spinach and ricotta parcels with sweet chilli sauce, mixed paella and Eton mess. Delicious!

19.30

Everyone is so eager to get to the kitchen as soon as Mum announces food is ready. Ava is looking at me and sniggering but I shake my head and raise my eyebrows as if to warn her not to grass.

'Kate this all looks amazing!' My aunty says all excited. And it does, there's a huge spread of lasagne, salads, coleslaw, mini sausage rolls, a selection of dips and of course the curry.

Once everyone is sitting down with their food, it falls silent. I love the concentration when people eat. Dad is the first to notice the spice.

'Woah! This has a kick to it,' he chokes.

My uncle is sitting at the end of the table, sweating profusely. 'I didn't want to say anything Kate but wow!'

Chloe burst out laughing 'This is the spiciest thing I've ever eaten!' Tears are streaming from her eyes.

Ava is nervously laughing and nudging me. Bless Mum, she's panicking and apologizing, whilst justifying that she only put the ingredients that it said on the recipe.

'It said one teaspoon of chilli powder and 1 tablespoon of paprika, I'm not sure what I done wrong.'

Aww I feel sorry for her now, I feel so bad. Everyone is so polite and just tucks into the lasagna which is amazing.

When dinner is over, I feel so bad that I tell Mum to sit down with a glass of wine whilst Ava and I do the washing up.

I can hear them in the living room still laughing about how spicy the meal was.

'Did you see Uncle Alan's face, he was turning red,' Chloe laughs. 'Where is my Dad?' She adds.

'He had to step outside, he was sweating so much,' Ava joins in.

It's become a good talking point to start the evening of drinking and fun.

23.00

This is a great night, great food, great company and the secret Santa went down well. I got a really nice bracelet 'from Santa', who I later found out was from my Grandad, so I thanked my Nan because there is no way he chose a bracelet that nice. Men don't do the shopping in my family, lazy things. Hansel loved his beer and we all had a bit of the caramel vodka which seems to be having an effect on everyone.

This is the 3rd time Mum has tried to calm the party down by asking everyone if they want tea or coffee but no one is listening. Red wine and Guinness still flowing.

When I look at my phone, I have 5 messages (always a nice feeling). Three from Brad and two from Regina George (Which is a WhatsApp group including 4 girls from my previous job. If you have watched *Mean Girls* you will know why we named ourselves Regina. She's the main antagonist in the film.) Basically, if any man read what was in there, they would be horrified at what we say about them. However, it is also hilarious and a bit of harmless fun!

Today we are demolishing any reputation Liam had. Liam is a guy Rosie met a few weeks ago at a house party. He was such a nice guy, a bit of a cheeky chap. They had a laugh, kissed a few times and swapped numbers…THEN! He turned into the world's biggest drip! Within a week he had bought her a ring (not an engagement ring but still), asked her for dinner with his parents and when she tried to let him down gently he said if she wasn't interested in a relationship then maybe they could be 'Winter Buddies', which is definitely the funniest thing we have ever heard it being referred to as. I don't think it worked as she has just sent a text to say she went on a date with another guy today who asked if he could wear joggers. Seriously! WHAT? Don't ask your date what outfit to wear, that is too embarrassing.

I think Mr Chow won on the presents. Brad bought him a new running ball and bought himself a pack of Terry's Chocolate Orange pieces. I'm not sure I would have bought myself chocolate after all those packets of crisps, which he is now on pack 6, only 4 more to go! Oh, by the way I forgot to mention, he was wearing a red checked shirt in the photo he sent earlier of him cleaning his teeth, so now he only has to tell someone he loves them.

03.00

This lot are wild! One of my Dad's sisters is nicknamed Aunty Hangover (for obvious reasons) but she is also a living legend. Once Chloe invited her new boyfriend along to one of these family get-togethers and Aunty Hangover (her mum) drank so much red wine and attempted to cartwheel through the garden. Chloe was mortified but it was hilarious, she is amazing, someone you always want at your party.

Tonight, Nan has got the whole clan up doing a line-dancing routine she has been learning at her classes on Wednesdays, Dad is doing shots of Tequila with the boys and Chloe started a game where you hold a broom upside down in the air and spin 10 times, then put the brush on the floor and try and stand on it. Jack got so dizzy he nearly pulled the Christmas tree down and Grandad had to steady him to the floor. What a night!

I can see my phone flash with a text, and attempt to make it over to the table where I left it earlier. It reads:

So, let's gloss over this before you call me a melt, you have helped turn this year into a wicked one, and for that I love ya Biatch!

Yeah, he's right, he is a melt. And pretty sure that's cheating but I have a hangover already and need to sleep.

Night guys!

31st December

NEW YEARS EEEVVVE!

09.45

I know its overrated but I love New year! I love the count down, the parties and the feeling of thinking that tomorrow is the start of this crazy amazing life where I'm going to be skinny and rich by March. So today is going to be spent building up to this big moment.

We are all up reasonably early, I don't feel as bad as I should after all those sambucas but I did accept Mum's offer of a tea towards the end. Aunty Hangover is living up to her name and we are all dining out on some bacon sandwiches cooked by Dad because Mum refuses to mess up any more meals (sshhh, she still doesn't know).

After saying all our goodbyes, Jack and I head off to sort the tyres out on my little banger. I need to cherish these moments as this time next year I will own an Audi R8 and will probably have my own mechanic as well as a chef and a housekeeper. I will also buy a scratch card to fund this expensive lifestyle because I'm not sure I want to work for it.

We finally made last minute New Year's plans with Jack's brother, Alfie, along with his girlfriend Samantha and her pals. The plan is to head up to a bar in London and have a 'few' cocktails. I have promised myself I will not do shots tonight because I get too carried away. Also, I doubt the bar we are going to does a 'three for a fiver' deal like good old Weatherspoon's.

12.13

Just had my tyres changed and we're now in the queue for a drive through McDonalds. Next year I won't be eating any unhealthy food and I suppose my personal trainer will be quite strict with me so have to have my last one now. We slowly drive up to the machine:

'Can I take your order please?' the woman on the tannoy asks.

'Yes, two BigMac meal's please, one full fat coke, one coffee and a side of cheese bites please.'

We find a space in the car park and wait for our meal.

12.25

Well that was amazing but also quite sad, I will miss food like that but it's a sacrifice I have to make to have my dream body. I once heard that it never tastes as good as feeling good feels and that is what I am now going to preach to myself from now on.

Now time to go home and chill before tonight's fun.

16.15

Arghhhh! Why am I so unorganised? Samantha just called to ask what I'm wearing. What am I wearing? Jeeez, how have I not planned this?! I know New Year is coming around as it comes around every year. I have been lazing about all afternoon. Right, first new year's resolution - be more organised.

I run to my wardrobe and start flinging on outfits but nothing fits. Why did I have that McDonalds?! I didn't need extra cheese bites. My favourite outfit - black jeans, and an orange vest top is in the wash….

Oh my God, I need something quick!

I slump on the bed and sigh. I need a plan. Oh, wait! New Look is open until 5… coat, keys…GO!

17.15

Don't laugh, but I'm now sitting in my car in New Look's car park having just got off the phone, crying to my Mum and telling her how I miss living with girls as I need someone to find me an outfit for tonight. Also, I need to borrow all my sister's makeup! I literally have nothing to wear. I feel fat, shouldn't have eaten that bacon sandwich for breakfast, and the McDonald's, and the candy floss crisps I bought just because they sounded odd, although they were actually very nice.

Thank God its New Year and everything is going to change tomorrow. In the words of Snoop Dog – I'll be toned, tanned, fit and ready!

20.20

OK so my melt down was a bit over dramatic, I found a pair of patterned leggings and a black lace top and now Samantha is doing my hair. It's so handy that Alfie's going out with a hair dresser! She's made it look amazing! I add a pair of red earrings and a splash of Cashmere perfume. Unfortunately, I don't own expensive perfume like Ava but it does the job.

Jack is in the kitchen making prosecco and brandy cocktails…Legend!

'To a great New year!' Samantha shouts and we call clink glasses and drink. Then head out….

23.15

It's 45 minutes until the count down and Samantha, her friend, Hannah and I have popped into the toilets for a quick freshen up. We left the boys at the bar to get the next round in and a few more shots! (I know what I said, but Sambuca is too tempting) We are just having a heart to heart when another girl comes in and screams 'Woahhh! We're half way thereee…!!' And in unison all 15 girls in the toilets scream 'Woahhh living on a prayer!' And this is why I love the girl's toilets. GIRL POWER!

23.59

It’s time!

10

9

8

7

6

5

4

3

2

1

HAPPY NEW YEAR!!!!!

The bar staff pop some champagne and jump up on the bar, spraying it everywhere! Everyone is hugging one another, wishing them a Happy New Year, even if they don’t know each other. So much love, happiness and hope in that one very moment! I love it!

Now time to celebrate! The music gets louder and we hit the dance floor.

03.20

Home. We made it!

Best night ever! So many cocktails, So much Sambuca!

We left at 2am it’s taken us sooo long to get back but we did stop to get a kebab.

I love Samanthaaaaa! She's so fun! We danced and danced. I'm so drunk and need to get some water. My feet are killing me.

It takes me ages to get into bed. Jack came straight in and put a pizza in the oven then passed out on the sofa. I went to turn the oven off but tripped over and fell into the kitchen door…what a mess.

Ohh, I love New Near. This is going to be the best year ever!

2017 Let's do this!

First… I've got to sleep off these Margaritas.

Chapter 3 – Day One of the rest of my life

1st January 2017

10.30

2 Nurofen plus and 2 Paracetamols

My head kills and I know I said I wouldn't eat any rubbish but I really need a fry up. The thought of a kale smoothie right now is making me feel ill.

Jack is still asleep so I roll over and check my phone.

One message from Molly:

I'm so scared right now.... I'm pretty sure my head has shrunk!

What?!

Hahahaha good night then? I reply.

Elise don't laugh. It feels smaller when I hold it.

This girl is hilarious! She is definitely going to text me later to let me know that she isn't drinking again until her birthday…she does it every year. Her birthday is in May and she only ever makes it until 22nd April, mainly because it's my birthday and she can't resist coming out to celebrate.

I have had the best nights with Molly. She has a six-year-old son and so whenever she manages to find a babysitter, we dress up, drink Tequila, go to a club and dance until the light comes on. I missed her this New Year but I think she spent it with her sister, up in Northampton.

11.00

I have to go back to work tomorrow so I only have today left of the holidays, what can I do? I need to write a fitness routine to start tomorrow. Then I will go shopping and get really healthy food for the week, that way there is no possible way I can't get fit. I think I will search for local Zumba classes and maybe start doing yoga or meditation to find my inner zen.

First, I need a shower and a cup of tea. I text Samantha: *Fancy coming to the cafe for breakfast?*

12.05

Samantha let me down. She said she has had a bacon sandwich and is too hungover to come out for food so I am now in the smallest, most expensive pub in Essex, eating a £15 burger. So much for my healthy diet.

Jack has found me a seat right underneath the TV so that he can pretend that he is listening to me when he's actually just watching the game.

This pub is so flashy. Lots of men in light pink shirts, who have clearly been on the sunbed for too long. I can hear them talking about their flashy cars and grabbing wads of cash out of the back pocket of their Armani jeans. I can feel my eyes rolling into the back of my head.

I wanted to go for a walk, in an attempt to get my amazing beach body, but it is raining…again, so I sip my coke in a strop.

'Shall we pop into town later and have a look in the sales?' I ask, mainly for attention rather than an answer. But he just grunted something that sounded like an agreement but without looking away from the screen.

I sigh and grab my phone to text Brad: *How's Holland?*

I wonder what the national beer is in Holland…. I need to know this for when I start my dream beer stall. Google says *Heineken.* Great! That's easy to get. Ooo I fancy a Heineken now, I'm just popping to the bar, I'll be right back.

16.15

I finally managed to drag Jack shopping…because there was nothing else to do! Now I have a ridiculous amount of healthy food and a Spanish lessons CD because I have had a brain wave. If I speak another language, I will be able to speak to rich yacht owners in Spain along the docks. We can become pals and then I can start mixing with the rich and famous! They will be able to tell me the best yacht to buy and I can sail around the world.

Also, I can abuse Piero, or at least understand him when he abuses me! He is Italian but can speak loads of languages so he will be able to understand me.

I met Piero in my previous job and he is a crazy Italian flirt! We literally have never said a nice word to each other but still are good friends because he's outrageous, but fun. The week after I left that job, he got fired for being inappropriate, shame really, I always found him quite funny. He was never offensive.

18.10

Something hilarious just happened.

I went for a run. That's funny in itself but let me tell you the story.

I dug out a pair of actual fitness leggings I optimistically bought 2 years ago. With a lot of force, I wedged my legs and muffin top into them. I stretched, I practiced my breathing and I was ready! Jack offered to come with me but I said no because he is much fitter than me and I wanted to go at my own pace (which as you will learn is not very fast). I walked to the top of my road because I know people around here and I'm not stupid. Then I lightly started jogging. This isn't too bad I thought. Maybe I can run one mile and just take it one day at a time, build it up and then potentially enter a marathon this summer. Anyway, I crossed over to the other side of the road and turned down the street opposite because I know it's a downward hill. I picked up speed pretty quickly and I was off. Ok this is getting a little harder I thought but I can work through the pain. I realised I had forgotten about my breathing. Deep breath in, slow breath out, deep breath in… slow breath out… then I took a double breath in (oh shit) tried to pick it back up by breathing back out and ended up breathing in a triple breath. By this point I had lost the pattern all together and was frantically breathing short breaths. I was also sweating an unattractive amount. Then it happened! My ankle gave way without any warning and I fell off the curb and rolled into the road. Fuck! That hurt.

I was sitting there panicking about being in the middle of the road and trying to nurse my ankle by grabbing it and rocking back and forth (you that well known method all doctors tell you to do) when a man ran out from his house and shouted 'Oh love, are you ok? I saw that, it must have been painful.' All I could think was 'Oh God! He saw it!' How embarrassing.

'I'm fine, thank you,' I try and laugh.

But then his wife came running out with a glass of water and an ice pack. 'Oh, you poor love, shall we call an ambulance?' She said in the softest voice I have ever heard.

'Oh no honest its fine, I think I've just twisted my ankle but thank you,' I reply and try and hobble back up.

By this point two neighbours had come out to find out what the commotion was all about and I could feel my face gradually getting redder and redder. This was not the worst of it. Once I had finally got to my feet, I thanked everyone for their concern and started hobbling back in the direction of my flat (which by the way I can still see). Listen, I can't tell you who started it because there was no way I looking back but as I was walking up the road someone started clapping and then someone else joined in and gradually there was an actual audience clapping and cheering as if I had just finished the marathon.

When I got in Jack could not contain his laughter, he said he had watched the whole thing from our bedroom window and was going to come down and help me but said he didn't want to embarrass me anymore than I already had but that shows how far I was from the flat.

Now I am sitting here with a cup of tea and actually finding the whole thing hilarious. But maybe running isn't the answer.

20.00

After calling my mum to tell her the story I am starving and now making dinner. Tonight's dish is Vietnamese pho, with a side of spring rolls. We visited Vietnam a few years ago and it was honestly the healthiest country I have ever been to. It was the only holiday where I returned slimmer than I left. Tonight, I will write a list of targets to achieve by the end of the year and then I will work a way of how to get there.

Learn to speak fluent Spanish

Obviously lose weight (not by running)

Find things to do around this area and make some friends here

Find a way of making money other than my job

More importantly find a new job

Oh, I can't believe the Christmas holidays are over and I have to go back to work tomorrow.

Right, I can't dwell on the negative. I shall spend the rest of the evening working out how to avoid that road for the rest of my life and listening to my Spanish CD ready to become a sexy senorita… I might have just turned this day around.

Chapter 4 – Back to normality

2nd January

5.45am *Alarm*… Snooze

6.00am *Alarm* … Snooze

6.15am *Alarm* … Snooze

6.30am *Alarm* … Hmmm can I hit snooze again?

‘Are you getting up?’ Jack grumbles but also pulls me closer so I’m a bit confused as to what he wants to me to do?

‘I’m trying!’ I laugh as I crawl out of bed. Ahh, it’s freezing! We need to sort that bloody heating out. I grab my dressing gown and run to the bathroom, turn the hot tap on full blast and wait for the room to steam up before getting in the shower.

I can’t wait until I’m rich and can keep the heating on all night, and not have to get up for work at ridiculous o’clock! Although I would wake up with a headache and feel like I had woken up in the desert.

As I step out of the bathroom, wrapped tightly in a towel, the fire alarm sounds and it's deafening. Jack runs out of the bedroom, almost bumping into me. 'What have you done? Is there a fire?' he panics.

'No, it's just the heat from my fine-ass body' I wink and strut to the bedroom to get changed while he is frantically waving the steam away from the smoke alarm. Who puts a fire alarm right outside the bathroom anyway? It's a very strange design.

One thing I have learnt about living this far away from work is my ability to shower, dress, makeup and be out of the flat in 20 minutes.

I defrost my car, put my new Spanish CD on and I'm off on a very depressing drive.

08.11

Luckily for me not everyone is returning back today and the roads are quiet. I spoke Spanish all the way. Well, with breaks of Ricky, Melvin and Charlie now and again. They cheer me up in the morning and make me laugh so much. What a great job! Imagine spending the morning with your mates, listening to music and playing on-air games with the nation. Today's question of the day is - 38% of guys are turned off by women who do this. I'll let you think about that one. I've just arrived at work.

I work as part of small team along with Kathy and Tom in a big events production company. My job is to source and distribute equipment for events. Tom ensures everything returns in a good condition and arranges for it to be fixed if not. Kathy is the head of department and makes sure the whole thing runs smoothly. I don't mind the job but sometimes it gets quite techy and I spend a lot of my time blagging it.

As I walk into the freezing cold, open plan office, I can see Tom and Bill sitting there, not saying a word to each other, as per usual. They are the only ones in the office so I can't avoid them.

'Hi guys!' I chirp, flinging my bag under the desk, untangling the scarf from around my neck and slumping on the chair.

'Hi' Tom replies, but carries on typing. Bill just grunts and doesn't look up but I am not giving up!

'So how was your Christmas and New Year?' I carry on, ignoring the fact they obviously have no interest in talking.

'Meh' Bill grunts. OK I give up with him.

'How about you Tom?'

'Yeah, it was ok! Elise, there's a ton of emails in the inbox for you and maybe we should start on invoices first.'

IS THIS GUY FOR REAL?? We have all had two weeks off, it was Christmas and all they want to talk about is work! Honestly this is what I have to deal with 5 days a week.

I get my phone out of my bag and text Brad:

I can't believe you have taken the first day off, surely that's cheating.

He replies straight away:

I kind of wish I was there now. I have to get an 8 hour ferry trip back from Rotterdam and the cabins that we reserved on the way here have sold out so I have to sit in the communal area.

Ooo, what a snob.

12.30

I received quite a few schmooze Christmas presents from the suppliers before I broke up for the break, so I have been doing the follow up phone calls to say thanks. They are all very keen to talk about their holidays and how they finally got a break, how it was nice to spend time with family and, most importantly, that they have a new bit of equipment that they think we could benefit from. January is normally a quiet time for events, so suppliers like to come in for a 'catchup' but all they really want to do is beg it with the top dogs.

13.34

Finally, it's lunch. I have been starving for the past 45 mins but refuse to go on lunch any earlier because then the afternoon will drag.

Where can I go for lunch? Normally I go with Brad but seeing as he's not here, I might just text him to update him on how the day is going.

This day is torture! You're paying for lunch tomorrow to make up for being away. That's all.

Why don't you make yourself a list for tonight? he replies.

Oh, that's a good idea. Jack is going out to a game tonight so I should really make a few plans. Hmm, first I need sushi. Only supermarket stuff, I'm not that posh.

14.29

People in this car park now think I am mad. I have been sitting in my car with my Spanish CD on repeating 'Quiero una mesa para dos personas por favor' whilst shoving sushi into my mouth. I have also written myself a list for tonight:

Find a way of making £10 – because I feel like I need to start somewhere and once I have figured out how to do that I will know how to make more.

Cook a healthy dinner – Start my 'New year, new me' diet - I did actually get some salmon while shopping for sushi, so will keep it in the fridge at work for the afternoon.

Look for a holiday – Jack is getting a season ticket at Spurs this year which is his treat to himself and mine is China so technically we both still need a summer holiday. This is how I justify it.

Make one pair of earrings – Another little treat for myself or maybe someone else.

Read a chapter of 'Yes Man'. Just to chill really.

18.34

Nothing really to report on this afternoon but feeling like I'm winning at life. Journey in under an hour and managed to get petrol…BOOOM!

As I put the key in the door, the stairwell to my flats is pitch black. The communal lights normally automatically come on but today they haven't. Oh, dear God, this is scary and a little bit dangerous. I live three floors up and it's a long way in the dark.

I manage to get to my flat using the torch on my phone. Put the key in the door and the cold air smacks me right in the face. Jeeez! I run to the kitchen and switch on the heating.

The feeling of success from the drive home has disappeared and then I realise I have forgotten to get the bloody salmon out of the staff fridge and I haven't defrosted anything else. I rummage through the freezer and find cod in parsley sauce which you can cook from frozen. Hmm what else can I have that's healthy but quick! I have a lot to do.

Couscous, roasted veg and asparagus. I start cooking and while I wait, I text Brad:

I'm am sick of being this cold and now the stairwell light is out.

Set the timer on your boiler then, he suggests.

As if I know how to set the timer on my boiler. I'm bored of his stupidity and I'm in a grump.

I need to eat my dinner before I do anything because that's probably why I'm so moody.

While the dinner is cooking, I set up my work station. Jack is out until around 11 o'clock so I can get beads EVERYWHERRRE! I've decided to make a small figure of a woman out of beads. Just a little idea I saw in Camden a few months ago and they look so cool.

The oven timer is finally going off so I am going to eat dinner, speak soon.

19.55

OK, the little figure earrings are harder than I first thought and the pendant I eventually made was too big for earrings, so I made it into a keyring, sent a photo of it to Molly who is also into crafty things and she said she loves it.

Wow are you going to sell them? She asks.

Well I tried to sell my jewellery and it didn't go down too well, maybe I will have it for myself! I reply.

No! Give it to me! I love it I will pay you £5 for it. She offers. Aww she's a good pal.

No! you can have it for free, I wouldn't charge you!

Wooo really? That's amazing, let's plan a night where you can come round and you can bring it then. I love it! Thank you!

Maybe it is worth £5. I could make a few and sell them online. What a great evening! I'm going to start an online business but I don't want this to be my way of making £10 so I will carry on with this and then find another way.

21.30

I made 4 keyrings, one was dressed in a skirt and hat, one had dress and belt, one had a handbag and then I tried to make one in the shape of a man but didn't work as well. Quite proud of myself actually.

Now I have to find a way of making £10. I have always wanted to invest so I might look into the best ways of investing.

I know there is an app on my phone for stocks and shares, maybe that will have more information.

21.45

Right, so I know this technically doesn't count as making £10 tonight, but I remember my Mum saying her friend buys premium bonds. She said she puts money away each month and wins every now and again, so I called NSCI and bought £500 worth. Eventually I will make back my £10, maybe more, and get rich. I didn't actually have £500 but I took some money from my savings as I think this is a worthwhile investment.

Next, I need to find a holiday. I normally have a very clear idea of where I want to go but apart from China, I have no idea. I text Jack an hour ago and he said we should look at Portugal. I haven't really ever thought about Portugal but I suppose its somewhere I haven't been and I got a scratch map for Christmas, which, if you don't know what one is, it's a map of the world in a gold colour. The idea is when you have visited a country you scratch it and it goes a different colour. Sounds great, doesn't it? But not when you are already obsessed with travel and have now realise that your 6-month round the world trip, numerous holidays with family and pals has not even scratched the surface (excuse the pun).

Argh! So confused, I'm normally so good at this but I can't seem to find the best place to stay…sod it, I'm leaving it until tomorrow at least I have chosen a country. I'm going to bed to read a chapter of my book and wait for Jack to come in.

Buenas Noches x

3rd January

13.50

This is a much better lunch. Actually, this is a much better day.

Tom is being a bit more talkative. Brad is back in and we have decided on Shakshuka for lunch. There is this Jewish café on the high street and they make the best Shakshuka!

We have been chatting away about Christmas, New year, the lists and just other random chit chat. Did you know peanuts are not actually a nut and are actually the oval seed of a tropical South American plant? We have been arguing about it for the past 10 minutes as I didn't believe him… turns out it is actually true and I now have to pay for lunch!

I have been telling him all about my round the world mobile bar idea. The idea is that when you go to a food festival and there is a paella stand, Chinese food, Thai noodles, Lebanese wraps etc. I will have a bar selling a beer from each country. Brad seems to think it's a great idea, which is weird because everyone normally laughs off my business ideas. To be fair, I come up with a lot of ideas. First there was my bouncy castle career, weekly speed dating events mission and of course my jewellery shop dream. He has been researching beers from around the world and we have been ranking them 1 to 10. However, this also means we are now late back from lunch and Kathy is definitely going to be in a strop with me.

Kathy and I have a weird relationship where she kind of hates me.

17.15

The day is going so slowly. I have 15 mins until I am free and can meet Graham, Natalie and Tanya for dinner. We have been debating about what to eat all day and have decided to go for Italian. It's easy isn't it? Everyone loves a pizza or pasta! Obviously, I will be getting salad because I am a skinny bitch now.

Before Brad left, he said he had nothing to do and asked for a list… hmm, what can I put on this list. I need to have a think…

18.45

Waiting for Graham outside Zara, as I went for a little bit of a late-night shop to pass time. Trying to think of one more thing Brad can do. So far, I have:

Try on a skinny-leg pair of jeans - because he is always wearing baggy clothes and reckon, he could pull the skinny-look off.

Join a dating site and spend at least 15 minutes on it. - I have never used one, I've been in a relationship with Jack for 8 years but I used to mess around setting Rosie up on dates when I worked at my previous job. Once she swiped left on this ridiculously good-looking man and he was a barrister and I got a bit too into it and was screaming at her 'WHAT IS WRONG WITH YOU!'

She looked so confused and said 'I don't like coffee?'

EH? 'What are you talking about? Why would you need to like coffee?'

'He is a barrister and would stink of coffee when he came home.' Oh, good god what is she talking about?

'WHY? Barristers are not known for drinking coffee!' I was so confused.

'Yes! But he will be making coffee all day so will come back smelling of it!' OH! Jeeez this girl.

'THAT'S A BARISTA!' I shouted with an Italian twang. She looked at me horrified and tried to find him again but never did.

Back to the list, I need one more. He keeps saying he wants to go ice skating but has no-one to go with so I might suggest doing that and then he will *have* to find someone to go with.

19.15

O*h wow! What is wrong with my jeans?!* he replies. *I can't wear skinny leg jeans. They're too tight! And where am I going to find jeans at this time of night?*

Oh, for goodness sake why is he so whiny.

You don't have to buy them. Just find some and try them on. It's late-night shopping tonight in town, or, if not, go to a 24-hour supermarket or something, I reply.

Ok, Ok fine! I will! Also, I have no-one to go ice-skating with but I will go on my own. This is going to be sad!

*Oh jeeeez, don't you dare go on your own. Ok change of plan. Text my mate Molly! 078454122***

WHAT!? You want me to just text your mate who I have never met and never spoken to? Well that will be odd. What would I say?

It's fine, she will love it.

Right! I need to text Molly and warn her.

Don't freak but I gave this guy at work your number as I dared him to text you, don't ask, just reply. Also, how's your tiny head?

She texts back instantly. O*k, and yeah, it's ok now. It grew back haha.*

She is literally the only person that doesn't question my madness. I love her for that!
I wonder what he is going to say?

22.30

Just got home. I do love living in Essex and having our own place but all my pals live so far away so I have to leave so early to get back at a reasonable time on a week night. What a good night though. We had so much fun, I had an amazing chicken and broccoli pasta… delicious and under 600 calories! I chose from the skinny menu.
I'll give a you an update on Brad's list: I received 2 photos earlier

of the pairs of skinny jeans he had tried on and they really suited him. I get he has his own style but they look good too. He normally wears baggy jeans, a pair of Van's, a t-shirt with an open shirt over the top. It's a good look but this is just something different. He didn't buy them but agreed that he actually didn't mind them. The photos were of him posed like a model so I think he liked them more than he let on.

He also set a profile up on a dating site and said that he thought it was a laugh but he doesn't think that he will get any matches. Worth a shot though! I wonder how he described himself? There is no way he would tell me and I don't blame him. It would definitely get sent straight to Regina. Why are girls like that? We feel the need to screen shot our messages from guys and tear them apart.

Talking of screen shots, Molly text me with a screen shot of the message that Brad had sent her:

Hi! So...Elise gave me your number. It's Brad, her friend from work. She obviously felt you didn't mock her enough so sent you some weird bloke with a book of bad jokes ... what are your thoughts on ice skating?

WHAT? Oh jeeez!

She texts me again seconds after. *Wait! You're not trying to set me up again are you Elise?*

Hmmm, no and yes really. I don't think they will suit but they are both single and could start talking. She needs a nice guy as she has the worst taste in men!

Well no, but carry on talking to him, he's a nice guy. I finally reply.

Oh yeah because 'nice guys' are my type. Sarcastic cow.

Anyway, I should really go to bed I have to get into the early night's routine again. It's so boring.

Buenas Noches!

7th January

14.30

So today I finally booked China! Booked the 'Dragon trip tour' which involves the Great wall of China (we couldn't get the camping on the wall one because apparently it too cold in March.) We get to eat in this restaurant that is famous for its Duck pancakes, trek though the rain forests and sip champagne at the top of a sky bar in Saigon. How cool is that?! I'm soo EXCITED! 9 days away in China with one of my best friends. It's going to be amazing. I'll miss Jack but think he said he is going to do DIY around the flat because he said I always moan that it's boring haha. To be fair it is!

We arranged to sort the visas out next Friday, so I am now in the shopping centre trying to work out how to use this photo booth. It's so bossy – put your head here, don't smile, no glasses, no hats.

Well this would be a very difficult game of 'Where's Wally'.

When I am finally happy with the photo (well I wasn't but the machine told me I had run out of attempts) I pressed print and it charged me an extortionate amount of money for a photo that made me look like a mad axe murderer. I then waited ages for it to print only to realise it had come out on the outside of the machine for everyone in the queue to see… well how embarrassing.

18.00

When I get home, I see that Molly has sent me a text: *I want to go to Ireland for my birthday. Will you come with me?*

Oh bejeez. I can't, I have just spent £900 on a tour and flights to China but I am so bad for saying no when it comes to a holiday…

I have just booked a trip to China so probably shouldn't.

As *if! You're Elise Smith and you are going to say 'yes' anyway.*

Shit! *Ok sold! When and where? Dublin?* Told you I wouldn't be able to pass up a holiday.

Na, it's too touristy.

You ARE a tourist...

But I want to see the beauty of Ireland not just the pubs.

Is she for real? That's what Ireland is all about.

Oh, who cares! I've been there before and it's her birthday so she can choose I suppose.

She texts her Mum and asks if she can look after her little boy for a few days, and the answer is yes, so it's all confirmed. Now I can start looking at more holidays. Woohoo! Still need to book the Portugal holiday with Jack but I don't know which is the best place to stay.

23.00

I have spent the evening looking at hostels in Dublin because I have persuaded her to stay there and travel out. She wants to hire a car and go to The Giants Causeway. I googled it…its rocks! ROCKS! Why, would you want to see Rocks? Oh, sod it, let's do it anyway. One week in and I have already booked two holidays, see told you 2017 would be amazing! Just need to get skinny and rich. I'm sure those premium bonds will make me some money.

I have also spent the evening looking at popular street food stalls so I can get an idea of all the beers I can sell on my dream beer stall, maybe one day I will do it.

Chapter 5 – Right back at ya!

18th January

08.30

Oh God I have been so lazy with writing but today will be worth writing about. So, you know I have done a few lists and given a few to Brad. Well, last night I thought I might text my Mum with one and see if she wants to join in.

I didn't explain much, I just told her the rules: *I have a list of tasks for you to do tomorrow. You can do them in any order you want but they have to be done by 12am tomorrow night:*

Read a chapter of a book

Make dinner using an aubergine

Make a short song with Ava

Take a landscape photo at night

Buy Dad a beer beginning with K

Wear earrings and a necklace

Phone/text someone you haven't in 6 months
Make a plan for tonight!

She didn't text back straight away so I assumed she had gone to bed or just thought the whole thing was ridiculous. But this morning she has text me back saying:
Right back at ya! This is yours:
Stroke a Dog
Listen to an Adele song
Watch a musical
Sit for an hour with the door of your front room open
Cancel a plan

WHAT! I literally can't stand all of those things, I have a fear of dogs, Adele is not my favourite singer (I know unpopular opinion), musicals are irritating and drive me mad, I avoid cancelling plans with people as I don't like letting people down and the door thing is a weird habit I have where I always have to have the door shut. Hmm, this wasn't meant to be a list of stitch ups.

Sod it, I can do this! This is my first list, apart from the one I did for myself so now I have to put my own theory to the test.

Jack's Mum has a dog and I could go over there tonight. However, that dog doesn't like me very much and avoids me at all costs. I will text my cousin Laura who lives a 3-minute walk away from my Mum, but I never get round to seeing her, so it will be nice to do that after work.

Hi Laura, Are you around tonight? Just for half an hour or so? Mum has given me a list of challenges and one is to stroke a dog... weirdest thing ever...I know

She texts back straight away. *That's hilarious! You're always welcome... come around for a cuppa!*

Perfect! That's one ticked off. Now for this musical. Hmm which, one could I watch…I do have Netflix and I'm sure there is one on there.

17.35

When I turn up at Laura's, Maisy opens the door with her hands behind her back, giggling. A slightly taller, blonde girl is behind her looking nervous but also giggling.

'Hi Maisy, is your Mum in?' I ask. Maisy is Laura's daughter but although she's nine and I have known her since she was born, I'm still not sure she knows who I am.

'MUM! Ava's sister is at the door!' Which proves my point! She knows I'm Ava's sister but doesn't know my name.

'Come in Elise! I'm just in the kitchen!' Laura shouts.

When I walk through to the kitchen, Ruby, the eldest of Laura's daughter's is in the kitchen trying to convince her Mum that Snapchat is not dangerous and that you can now add cat ears to your selfie. Don't ask, I've never understood it! Anyway, she wasn't convinced and so Ruby and her friend storm out of the room and upstairs.

'Hi Elise!' We touch cheeks and make kissing noises while hugging. I don't get why people do it, so odd.

'Casper is upstairs with Maisy, what is all this about then?' She asks whilst filling the kettle.

I explain about the lists and that I have 24 hours to complete them. I'm not sure if she is impressed or confused.

'CASPER! Look who's here to see you…' She speaks in that weird way dog owners talk to their pets as if they were babies.

Casper comes bounding down the stairs, obviously being mis-sold a treat and she grabs him before he gets to me as I think I would have screamed and run through the patio windows. Laura puts him on the table just as Ruby comes in with a camera ready to photograph this very strange moment.

As I stroke the fluffy, white fur, Casper looks back at me with

'Look how embarrassing you look' eyes, licks his lips and jumps off the table. Well at least that's over! Ruby's friend whispers (very loudly) in Ruby's ear 'Is she a bit weird?'

I am about to answer 'Erm no I'm not a bit weird and by the way you have ketchup on your face,' when Laura asks if I want tea or coffee and the girls run off.

We then chat for a while about the flat and Jack, all the usual stuff and then she says 'How is Ava? Has she been in any shows recently?' Ava is an up and coming actress/ dancer.

'No, I don't think so, I know she went for a few auditions last week and I think she has a few extra parts coming up but nothing major at the moment.' I explain and take sip of my tea.

'Have you seen that new musical La La Land? It's just come out in the cinema? I bet Ava would love that.'

'No, I haven't actually. Is that out now?' Because then it suddenly dawns on me, that is the musical I could see tonight! Jack will hate it, but so will I, so we can hate it together! I text him straight away: *I'm taking you to the cinema tonight…my treat.*

I finish my tea say my goodbye's and head home.

20.00

It took a bit of persuasion but I finally got Jack to come with me. I mean I understand how odd that would have sounded, I have been ranting for 8 years about how I can't stand musicals and now I'm taking him to one and calling it a treat. I had to explain the lists thing quite a few times because he didn't understand why I had asked for a list of things I hate. I told him that wasn't the point but it's how Mum read it so maybe I should give it a go. Anyway, we are now late for the film but oh well not too bothered about missing the whole thing to be honest.

'Two tickets for Lala land and the extra-large popcorn and Coke please,' I try and say in an enthusiastic way but I am not looking forward to this.

'Woah, you're pushing the boat out Elise. That's going to cost a fortune,' Jack whispers, so we don't look cheap in front of the lady at the counter.

'We are going to need it; it's going to be a long night,' I whisper back and nudge him towards screen 4.

22.45

It was exactly the reason I don't like musicals! It started great, a bit of an obvious girl meets boy scene and just when they are about to confess that they might quite like each other … THEY SING IT! Tap dancing all over the place. We both sigh at the same time, he turns to me and mouths 'Really?' and we burst out laughing.

Back in the car now and I realise I haven't listened to Adele yet.

'Jack can you find 'Someone like you' up on YouTube please and play it'

'Eh? But you don't like that song,' he states quizzingly.

'I know but Mum has put it on the list.'

'Fair enough.' And he puts it on, shaking his head.

As soon as it starts playing, I can't help it I feel really sad and tears jerk to my eyes. I can barely see the road. Jack is looking at me very confused.

'Elise you don't need to make yourself this sad, it's crazy!' But it's done now and I had ticked off the whole list apart from keeping the door open which I figured I could do tonight when I go to sleep. Oh, and to cancel a plan hmmm…

23.25

When we get in, I text Mum to let her know that I had competed my list and ask how she got on with hers?

She said she had done all of them apart from make dinner with an aubergine, which is pretty easy when you think about it.

'Oh, and also Mum I can't come around Tuesday, I'm busy!' Haha, two can play that game.

19th January

07.12

Aww, it was so nice seeing Laura yesterday. I really should go and see her more often. And I completed my first list! It was actually fun, not what I would have chosen but it wasn't as bad as I thought it would be.

Now for Mum's pay back. What can I put on her today's list that she won't like?

Eat a banana (Mum can't stand bananas and, when we were younger, she used to tell us she was allergic to them so we would still eat them).

Don't Google anything for 2 hours after dinner (she's famous for the line 'Ohh let me Google that' at the end of dinner about ANY subject).

Call Nan (who hates Cats) and tell her how much you love Cats... that should cause some drama.

Right now, I need to get to work. I'm going to be so late, but I'm only working half day today because I need to go and sort the visas out.

13.30

Graham and I meet at the station and head for the Chinese Embassy. When we arrive, there is a massive queue and everyone looks freezing cold as if they have been standing there for hours. We take our place and start discussing all the things we need to get and do ready for our trip.

'We need to learn some Chinese phrases to get us around when we arrive,' he suggests.

'Yeah that's a good plan actually! All I know is, how to say 'bèn dàn' which means stupid egg.'

'Stupid egg?' He looks confused.

'Yeah, I think its like an insult for fool or idiot.' I shrug.

'Ok, we seriously need to learn more phrases then,' he laughs.

After queuing for what feels like forever, we are finally allowed in. We get to the desk and the lady asks 'Which hotels are you staying in, please?' She looks so stern.

I hand her the itinerary and explain that we haven't booked the hotel for our first night yet because we want to get the visas sorted first. But she wasn't having any of it. We are sent over to this little booth with laptops and have to book a hotel there and then. There is a 5-minute slot so we scrabble around and find one that is in our price range, book it and run back to the desk with the details.

She grabs the piece of paper with our booking on it, looks straight back at us and sighs as if we are wasting her time but then she processes our application and we're told to wait 1-2 weeks for our passports with Visas to be sent in the post.

As it's only 14.45pm and we are in London we go to the pub to celebrate. Why is midday drinking on a weekday the best type of drinking?

19.19

Just arrived back home after being stuck on the trains in rush hour and received my first text from Mum. I thought she had given up on the idea.

Just text Nan saying how much I love Cats and thinking of getting one... she hasn't replied!

Ooo that won't go down well.

Haha have you eaten a banana?

Yes, but it was vile. She sent a photo of her eating a banana with a very distressed face!

Have you had dinner yet? Remember you can't go and Google something after!

Ava is cooking at the moment because I had to work late but I am Googling now to get my fix.

That might be cheating!

What you gonna do about it, Ginge?

Haha what attitude! Does your mother talk to you like that?
I might try and drag Jack out for a walk, I feel pretty hungover from the vodka and coke I was drinking earlier.

20.00
This is unbearable. What am I meant to do for 2 hours without going on the computer?

See, she is addicted.

G*o for a walk.* I suggest.

But we have been talking about the seven wonders of the world and we can't think of the last two and I'm desperate to find out!

No, you can't, just go for a walk or something! Or call someone for the answer

I think I will, Nan still hasn't replied.

22.04

On our walk, I find out there are a few yoga classes just up the road and there is one on a Tuesday. Maybe I should try that. We also live quite close to a massive park; how did I not know this? I need to explore this place more.

Mum text back and said that she called Nan and she answered the phone saying 'Why are you thinking of getting a cat? I hate Cats! Funnily enough Kate, I was thinking of getting a pet wasp!' Hahaha Mum hates wasps. She said it was hilarious at how angry she was, so Mum explained the lists and Nan found it funny in the end and said it was a good idea. Also, she seemed to know the seven wonders of the world. What a legend!

I LOVE LIST LIFE!

22nd January

06.30 – I know, a disgusting hour but its Monday and I have work.

Last night I was lying in bed and asked a half asleep-Jack for a list but he said he was tired and couldn't think of anything and then mumbled something about Spurs, he obviously wasn't really listening to me. So, I sat up with an unexpected burst of energy and text Brad and asked him for one.

He text back straight away: *Oh, you want one this time, do you? I thought it was a stitch up for me. Right here goes*:

Eat a fruit or vegetable you have never eaten before

Learn how to count to 5 in another language

Tell Ava something you love about her

Choose something to do with me outside of work

SET YOUR BLOODY HEATING TIMER!!

Say the word 'Unbelievable' 6 times between 10am and 1pm

Oo, that's a solid list!

07.45

On my way to work and the 'Question of the day today is - 84% of people admit to only doing this once a year?'

If you know it please let me know it's been driving me mad the whole journey and when they announced the answer, I was in a tunnel so it cut out.

08.30

When I get to work, I make a cup of tea whilst trying to think of something I can tell Ava I love about her… Hmmm:

*I love how cool your big sister is…*does that count? No? Ok I love it when I come in drunk and you look after me so I'm not so bad in front of Mum and Dad. OK. No!

*I love that you always look after me when I'm feeling ill, or drunk...*send!

She used to look after me all the time when I had had too much to drink. Once, I went for a walk with Natalie and our pal Louise. It was a Sunday night and it was meant to be a Sunday stroll. We started walking towards the park but at the other end of the park was the town centre. It was 8.00pm and we were heading towards the high street. One of the promoters asked if we wanted to go into the bar for a free shot (standard) so we did! But the hustle worked and when we got to the bar, they offered us a bottle of wine for £6 and we thought *ahh why not!*

After a few glasses/bottles, we decided we should head home. Turns out we are weak when it comes to shots so as soon as we stepped outside, we got lured into another bar and ended up having another few bottles! Anyway, one thing you will learn about me is I cannot handle wine! Natalie and Louise had to practically carry me home.

When I got in, my parents were in bed and Ava was the only one awake! She got me toast, made me tea (both didn't stay down) then tucked me into bed and wedged a pillow behind my head so I didn't choke! And when Mum got up to find out what all the commotion was about and shouted at me for being noisy, she lied and said I wasn't feeling well. So yes, I love her for that!

09.34

I have been at work for an hour and a half, had 2 cups of tea, eaten four Jaffa cakes out of pure boredom and replied to zero emails. Brad came in about five minutes ago and is looking at his watch waiting for 10am. Steve is grunting about the traffic. He arrived half an hour ago! I mean how is this still bothering him?

Steve is a middle-aged misery and I call him the king of ists and ic's because he's sarcastic, sexist and all other ists and ics you can think of. He uses the world 'Unbelievable' to describe everything! So, Brad thinks it's funny that I will have to join him on this UNBELIVEABLE rant. I squint my eyes at Brad and shake my head. It's dead silent in there and the sound of my typing is annoying Bill… again.

09.59

One minute to go…

10.01

I turn to Kathy, 'This weather is unbelievable isn't it?'

She looks at me whilst still typing, she has no expression whatsoever and then looks back at her keyboard. This is hard work. 'What I saw on the news was unbelievable this morning, did you see it Tom?' I never watch the news so this could go either way but I imagine what was shown this morning was unbelievable, I know Trump has just won the American elections so I think that's all still the hype. Tom didn't answer me anyway so, thank god, I didn't have to get into that.

10.13

'Brad, I think we should have the most unbelievable lunch today, what do you think?' Brad just holds up three fingers. OH MY GOD. Unbelievable is the most annoying word!

12.54

I smashed it! I managed to get the work 'unbelievable' in six times and guess what? Steve had the cheek to say 'Have you discovered a new word Elise? You seem to think everything is unbelievable today.' Is he for real?!

Anyway, Ava texts back: *Thank you Brad.*

Damn it was too obvious! Mum obviously told her about the lists.

14.45

Back late from lunch but I did get a pomelo. Not sure what it is but it looks like a grapefruit. I will eat that tonight for my 'fruit that I have never tried before.'

18.05

ARHGHH this traffic! It's so horrible and I'm freezing. I finally get in my flat and the light still isn't working in the stairwell. Oh bejeez, there are elderly people that live in these flats. How are they going to get up the stairs in this dark?

As soon as I get in, I run to the kitchen. Right! I need to set this bloody timer? I don't know how to set timers because I've never had a boiler before. Maybe I can call someone or Google it? Nope! I can do this. Plus, I think that's cheating.

I rummage around trying to find something that will tell me how to fix it and then there on top of the boiler, I spy a manual! Hmmm now let's see if this thing even works.

Page 3 – *If your boiler has a dial, set the clock to the right time.* Done! *Flick down the pins for when you want the heating to come on.* Right well we get up at 6.30am so maybe come on at 5.30 a.m. Then, we leave at 7.am so I'll leave the switches throughout the day. We come back at about 6pm and I am not having it off until 1am just in case we stay up late. Well, that should be it but I won't know until its actually on I suppose. Meanwhile I will wrap up warm and make a hot-chocolate to defrost.

I keep tapping the radiator to see if it has come on but it seems to still be cold. I'm not sure how long it takes to warm up.

19.30

After I have finished my hot-chocolate I tap the radiator and it's on! It worked! I actually set my timer! How embarrassingly exciting!

Ahh I can hear a key in the door, it's Jack! I can't wait to tell him! Oh, I'm so excited. I run up to him as soon as he gets in and do a 'I fixed the boiler dance' which kind of goes a bit like a one-man Mexican wave, whilst jumping from one foot to the other. He seems pretty impressed.

'I was thinking of getting George round to do that,' he says, whilst checking the boiler over in case I have damaged it in anyway. George is his oldest brother. No need for George, I am a genius!

Right, now! I haven't ever been out with Brad outside of work. I'm not sure why… just didn't really have a reason to I suppose. We see each other all day at work. I mentioned it to Jack just in case he had a problem with me going out for a drink with a random man from work but he didn't seem to be bothered. He's pretty good like that, I mean we have been going out for eight years, so he trusts me.

I text Brad: *Brad,* what *are you up to next Friday? Fancy going to the pub for a beer and burger?*

Sure, but you're paying because I just had to pay for my car to be cleaned and it was you that left all the sandwich wrappers and bottles in there.

Fine. I type, luckily, he can't see my rolling my eyes.

Sorted, that's most of the list done now. I just need to learn how to count to 5 in erm, let me think…Japanese? I think I will see if there is a lesson online. Flick open my laptop and type in the search- '*How to count to 10 in Japanese*'. The first result came up with a YouTube video and it's a crazy little song. Here goes…

22.54

Ichi

Ni

San

Shi

Go

Roku

Nana

Hachi

Ku

Juu

Ok I got carried away and got to 10 but the YouTube video had a great little tune so I was singing it round the flat, much to Jack's disgust.

List completed. Me voy a la cama, Buenas Noches!

23rd January

MORNING!!

I'm feeling refreshed, awake and ready to spread the List Life word.

Standing in the shower, I pull back the shower curtain and stare at the bright yellow wall in front of me. I have always wanted a bright yellow bathroom. I know it sounds weird but I used to see other people's bathrooms and think this would be better if it was a bright colour so you feel refreshed. Now I have my own bright yellow bathroom and I LOVE it! It wakes me up and makes me feel happy!

Oh yes! I forgot to say, my Mum text me last night to say that Nan had been asking about the lists and said that she has written me one so here goes:

Bake a Cake

Tell someone a joke

Make up a poem about a China man (a China man? Does she mean a Chinese man?)

Pray before you go to sleep

Yes! Nan is onboard. Nan and I are besties. I go around to her flat every week. She makes me dinner and we watch all the soaps. Sometimes we have a glass of wine or she makes tea from fresh tea leaves and we catch up on the week's activities.

She lives in a warden-controlled flat but has bagged herself a double so it's really nice and spacious. Nan is a crazy, amazing 84-year-old with a 70-somethingyear-old boyfriend who lives in the flat downstairs. I can't wait to do her list.

I start with the joke and I know just the person. My mate Harry! He sends me shocking jokes all the time and genuinely thinks they are funny. Again, we have been friends for years and to this day I don't know why or how we have lasted this long. He used to live around the corner from me and we hung around in the same crowd but now he lives down in Somerset with his girlfriend, who is wayyy out of his league.

Anyway…

Teacher to class: 'Whoever stands up is stupid.' Nobody stands up.

Teacher: I said, 'Whoever stands up is stupid'. Little Jimmy stands up.

Teacher: 'Do you think that you are stupid Jimmy?'

Jimmy: 'No Miss. I just thought you might be lonely being the only one standing up'.

I know, it's a rubbish joke but he will love it and I will have ticked something off the list.

12.30

Today's first achievement is I have mastered looking like I am working whilst writing a poem about a 'China man' as Nan requested. I think she means Chinese man or Man from China so this is my poem:

I met a man from China,
In my local Chinese diner,
He spoke about his day,
And how he used to live far away.
In a place called Shangri- La City,
Where he said the views were pretty.
He said he had a wife,
And loved the English life.
When my order was ready,
He said the spring rolls were veggie.
He said good bye Elise,
And threw in prawn crackers for free!
…Boom!

And Kathy didn't suspect a thing.

13.45

LUNCH TIMEEEEE!

Dragging Brad round Lidl's, trying to get ingredients for my cake. I don't bake. Ever! I once made scones and they looked amazing but when I tasted them and I hadn't put sugar in. I made a pizza that turned out like a pie and a pie that looked like a pizza so baking is not my best talent. I decided on a sponge cake with cream and strawberries. That can't be that hard can it? Brad's brother is a chef so he told me what ingredients to get.

14.45

When I get back into the office, Tom comes straight up to me with pursed lips and not looking me in the eye.

'Kathy would like to see you upstairs in the meeting room,' he announces.

Oh jeez, what have I done now? To be honest, I am 15 minutes late back from lunch and have been for the last 2 weeks. I put my bag down by my desk, take off my coat and head upstairs. Here goes…

17.15

I have to pull over. I can't see the road through my tears. I have lasted all day without crying but I can't hold it in any longer. I scramble through my bag to find my phone and call Mum.

'Hi Elise!' She chirps.

I can't talk, I'm crying so hard and trying to get my breath back.

'Elise? What's up? What's happened?' She sounds panicky now so I have to pull myself together.

'Mum, I HATE it there, I hate it!'

'Why what's happened?' She asks again.

'I got back from lunch and Tom said Kathy wanted to see me in a meeting room. I have been back from lunch late a few times this week so I knew I would be pulled up on that but after she had told me off for that she said: 'Elise, I have been speaking to senior management and a few issues have been raised about how much time you are spending with Brad. Is there anything going on between you?'

'WHAT! Senior management? Why would they be worried about that?' she shouts.

'EXACTLY! I mean nothing is going on we are just friends but why did she ask me like that? Why did she make it a big deal? I feel like I have done something awful!' I say through stuttered breath.

'I know. Is there something in your contract that says…?'

'And!' I interrupt. 'I speak about Jack and how we have just moved in together and anyway what has any of it got to do with senior management? If there was anything going on with Brad and ..' I'm angry now. I'm fuming in fact. 'What has it got to do with her or them? I understand it might look that way as we are always going to lunch together but that's because we are FRIENDS and no-one else speaks to me there! Also, why didn't she just ask me like a normal girl would, like try and get the goss, not bring me to one side and have a full-on meeting about it?!'

'Well don't tell Jack, it will make him feel bad. Just go home and have a nice evening and forget about it all.'

'Ok. Thanks Mum, sorry for being dramatic.'

'That's ok, I'm used to it,' she laughs, 'But it was wrong of Kathy to go about it in that way.'

I hang up, put my Maroon 5 album on full blast and sing every word all the way home and it helps. By the time I get home I feel fine. Good old Adam Levine!

18.05

I get in the door and text Brad straight away:

Did Barry say anything to you when you got back from lunch (Barry is his boss but is also 'Senior Management' so let's see what he has to say).

Yeah, he said he knows I am an adult but please try and keep to your set hours.

And…

And did he mention us?

Us?

As in what is going on between us? I feel embarrassed even asking him.

EH? What is going on between us?

Kathy dragged me into a meeting and first she said how late we have been blah blah blah... then she asked what is going on between you and me, I explain.

WHAT?!

I know, I'm livid!

Jesus! We are only going on lunch together and she knows you have a boyfriend. These people need to get a hobby. Are you ok?

No, I cried all the way home.

Oh Elise, I'm sorry, but don't worry about them, she probably fancies me haha. Anyway, what you got for dinner?

As if! But he's right maybe I have made a big deal out of it. I need to forget it now. Jack will be home soon and I need to act normal. Mum's right. There no point upsetting him over nothing.

19.00

I can hear Jack's key in the door and I just can't help myself. I can't keep anything from him.

'Kathy thinks something is going on with me and Brad and said that senior management have problem with it,' I blurt out, almost as soon as he has walked through the door.

He just laughed.

'Elise, you have always had male friends and you always get someone who thinks it's more. Don't worry about it. Anyway, what's for dinner?'

Is that all boys think about? Actually, I don't think it's just boys, I am normally the first to mention food but I haven't made dinner, all I have been doing is sitting underneath a blanket and feeling sorry for myself.

'Well, I have to make a cake so I will make a quick dinner.'

'A cake? Can you make cakes? Have we even got ingredients for cake?'

'Nan sent me a list and I have to make a cake, wanna help?' I ask.

'Na you're alright. We're playing Chelsea tonight.'

Technically he isn't playing anyone and is going to sit in his pants with a beer. Getting a sports channel was the worst idea EVER! I head into the kitchen and start making the cake.

20.30

Ok the top of the cake broke in two but it actually looked quite good.

Jack went to his Mum's to watch the game with Alfie in the end because I went on a 'too much football' rant, so I gave the cake to him to give to her - I won't eat that much cake anyway.

Right, I am going to get a bottle of wine from the shop next door and watch a chick flick while he is out.

20.45

'Hello Love,' The guy at the till says.

'Hi,' I chirp, and place the bottle of wine and cookies on the counter.

'No scratch cards today?'

How embarrassing, is that what he recognises me for? Oh, I need to sort my life out.

'No, not today, just the wine and biscuits.' I pay and get out of there quickly.

23.00

I ended up watching Pretty Woman because it's a classic and Jack is not a fan. Now I'm watching one of those programs where some high maintenance bride is trying to find her perfect wedding dress. On this episode she has her Mum and 3 bridesmaids with her and is looking for a diamante, fishtail style dress. The first few dresses she tried on were ok but now she seems to really like this one and we are all in suspense to see it…

'Nope!' I shout out loud to myself, as the bride struts out from the dressing room.

I can hear Jacks keys in the door, but it doesn't stop me, I'm zoned.

'Nope not that one. It's disgusting! You look ridiculous,' I'm ranting to myself.

When I look up Jack is standing there, laughing.

'Have you *seen* yourself, Elise?' He looks at the tv and then back to me. 'You are in a polka dot dressing gown, fluffy socks, glasses on and judging her outfit.'

Hmmm I look down at my dressing gown, brush the crumbs off me from where I had been eating cookies and downed the rest of my glass. 'Fair enough,' I laugh. 'How was football?' I ask but I'm not that interested.

'Yeah, was good. We won 2-1.'

'Wine? I have a glass each left?' I ask, whilst pouring myself one.

'Yeah, go on then. I'll watch the rest of this program with you.'

'Ok, but don't moan about it!' I snap '...unless it's about the dress. It's a revolting dress.'

23.50

Before I go to sleep, I kneel next to my bed and pray. Jack actually does it with me, which is hilarious. I'm not sure if he likes this list lark or whether he just puts up with me.

I recite the prayer my Nan used to say to me when we were little.

'In my little bed I lie,

Heavenly father, hear my cry,

Lord protect me through the night,

And keep me safe 'til morning light.'

Aww! I loved that when I was a kid. Nan lived what seemed like ages away but it was only a 45 min drive. Sometimes, she used to stay over. I would get home from school and see her big, blue, overnight bag and that meant she was staying. I would get so excited! She always went to bed at the same time as us and slept in mine and Ava's room on a pull-out bed. We sang songs which would annoy Mum and then, just before we went to sleep, she would make us say that little prayer.

But tonight, instead of singing songs before I go to sleep, I want to text Regina.

Girls, I have been doing a thing I like to call 'List Life'. I write you a list of 5 things to do and it has to be done within 24 hours - does anyone want me to give them a list.

Rosie texts back first: *What is this now? Do you ever just sit in front of the TV and do nothing? Why do you always have a new game?*

You didn't answer my question. Are you up for it or not? It will be fun.

No.

Hmm. Boring cow.

Ok, how about you give me a list?

Zee: *Much better idea. Ok. Get a picture with the wand' (I'll* explain later what she means).

Dawn*: Don't talk for an hour when Jack comes in.*

Zee: Wear a dress to work

Dawn: Learn how to do the Haka.

Rosie: *Don't swear all day. You have to give me 20p for every time you do*

Oh, this is going to be hard with those loons at work but ok let's do this!

I text Tom:

Tom, do you still have your crystal wand? If you do is there any chance you can bring it in tomorrow because I have been asked to take a picture of something spiritual and I thought that fits perfectly.

I know it's a lie but he doesn't need to know that.

Right finally, I'm going to sleep.

Good Night!

24th January

06.04

I start trying on dresses before I have a shower but only one fits.

It's black and floaty so hides all my lumps and bumps. I have wasted so much time faffing around and it's too late to have a shower, so I throw my hair up in a bun and will put my make up on in the car.

06.45

I get in the car and have to re-arrange my dress so many times to feel comfortable. I hardly ever wear dresses and NEVER to work.

08.23

I'm late! I'm hungry and I have sworn 3 times, to myself, but it still counts. I'm not doing this half-heartedly.

When I get to work, I scurry across the office and sit down and apologise for being late, even though I have already warned Kathy by text. She looks me up and down and is just about to say something bitchy about my dress when Steve walks in behind me doing his usual rant about the traffic. As soon as she sees him, she acts all chirpy, sits up tall and fluttering her eyelashes, as if she's purposely making a point that I have annoyed her.

One day just before Christmas we went for drink with some of the suppliers and she told them that she and Tom aren't really morning people and that when I started, they had to get used to me coming in asking about their evening and saying how it was a nice day! Jesus! What a bitch I am! How do they put up with me? (Crap! Does bitch count?) I was just sitting there awkwardly sipping my gin and tonic and trying not to roll my eyes.

Everyone has settled down now and is typing away silently, Tom arrives back from the kitchen with a cup of tea. He sits down and says (very loudly I might add):

'Hi Elise. Wow nice dress. Let me show you my wand!' WHAT! He did not just say that out loud!

It's the quietest office in the world and EVERYONE is now looking at me. Oh my God, this is so embarrassing. I shade my face and look down at the desk to avoid eye contact. The heat from my cheeks is burning. I glimpse up at Brad and he is biting his finger trying so hard not to laugh.

'Thanks Tom.' I whisper and quickly take a photo to send to Regina. Tom bless him is completely unaware of how cringingly embarrassing that situation was.

Basically, the reason Regina asked me to take photo of the wand is that Tom is really into spiritual stuff and carries around this crystal wand and says it heats up when there's high levels of energy in the room. He also claims he can talk to the dead which freaks me out. Anyway, I've told Regina about all this and they find it hilarious. Hence the wand photo.

09.45

I'm just working through a few emails when a cool breeze travels across the office and I suddenly realise, I am not wearing a bra!

I had all intentions of finding the right dress, then having a shower and getting ready properly but because it took so long, I just rushed out the house. How have I only just noticed this?

'Kathy, do you have any sticky tape please?' I have a plan.

She shakes her head but hands me a roll. I take a piece and run into the lady's toilets. I know this is not ideal but I have no idea what else to do. I run into a cubicle and cover my nipples with the tape because it's cold and my dress is quite thin.

I feel myself go red when I get back to my desk but no one is even looking up from their laptops.

10.15

'Shall we go and get a cuppa?' Tom asks.

'Oh yeah I could do with tea actually. Kathy? Would you like anything?' But she's on the phone so I take her cup and I'll make her one anyway.

When we get into the kitchen Tom is chatting away about his weekend plans and makes us both a drink.

'I'm just going to pop to the loo, I'll be back in a sec,' I tell him, leaving my tea on a shelf just in case someone decides to take it.

Whilst I'm in the toilet, I check my phone and search for an online tutorial of how to do the Haka, ready for tonight. There's quite a few so I save one, freshen up and head back.

I get back to the kitchen and Kathy is in there.

'Oh hi, I think Tom made you a coffee.' I explain and whip my tea from the shelf but it catches on the corner and what feels like slow motion the hot boiling tea pours all down my dress. 'Holy shit!' I scream and run back to the toilets. Kathy follows but is also calling someone from her mobile.

'Hi yeah can someone quickly come to the ladies, we have an emergency!'

Within seconds, two other ladies join us, Chrissy from HR and Helen from health and safety. They start shoving wads of paper towels under a running tap and order me to lift my dress up. Oh, this is not ok. I have no bra on and my nipples are taped down with sticky tape! How is this my life?

I lift my dress as high as I can without showing my boobs and they slap freezing cold, wet paper towels to me and wrap me in cling film. I did not wear my best knickers today and am avoiding any eye contact.

'We need to get you to A&E,' Helen says, whilst she is filling in an accident form.

'Really? It doesn't feel that bad?'

'It's the procedure, we have to follow the health and safety guidelines.'

'I'll take her!' Chrissy offers, but I think she just wants to get out of the office.

I thank everyone for their help and head towards Chrissy's car. I don't know Chrissy that well but she seems like a nice lady. She works upstairs so I don't work very closely with her. We start chatting about the weather and work and all the standard British ice-breakers and then when we have run out of things I gamble and decide to tell her about the no bra incident.

'What! So, you're not wearing a bra now?!' She chokes.

'Nope, and when all that happened, I thought you were going to think I was a right hussy.'

She laughed so much. 'Elise that is hilarious, let's hope you get a good-looking doctor when we get to the hospital.'

'Oh God, I forgot I have to do all that again.'

11.45

That was the quickest I have ever been in A&E. They examined me, said it was like sun burn so advised me to put cream or after-sun on it and said I will be fine, so we just got back and it was as if nothing happened, no one has even asked how I am.

13.45

Kathy tried telling me that I had already had a break (the hospital trip) so didn't need a lunch hour but I read my rights and won the war. I am waiting for Brad to come out of his meeting (because I'm refusing not to go to lunch with him despite the rumours. I might hold his bloody hand, that would get them gossiping but would also scare Brad.) Anyway, he doesn't even know I am back from the hospital yet. As soon as he sees me, he gasps.

'Are you ok?' He sounds genuinely concerned.

'Yeah I'm fine. They said to just use cream and the redness will go down. That teaches me for wearing a dress. Also, I have a drama I forgot to put on a bra this morning because I was in a rush and it was so embarrassing. Can you tell?'

'Elise, I'm a bloke, I noticed as soon as you walked in this morning,' he laughs.

'Oh God how embarrassing. Can we go into town and I will pick a cheap one up there and also I need to get some cheese for fajitas tonight?' I beg.

13.55

We are on our way to the shops and he randomly bursts in to uncontrollable laughter.

'What?' I join the laughter but I'm not sure what we are laughing at.

'Did you ask to see Tom Clarke's wand?' He's off again, red-faced and tears leaping from his eyes.

'BRAD! It's not funny! This is so embarrassing because they don't even know I'm doing this bloody list thing so they just think I asked to see his 'wand' or worse that I asked him to bring in a crystal wand. They now think I'm as crazy as him.'

'It was hilarious!'

14.34

I managed to grab a cheap, black bra from the supermarket and had all intentions of getting cheese. However, on the way to the fridge aisle I got distracted and ended up forgetting the cheese and buying some new orange flavoured vodka and a 3 for 2 deal on makeup instead. We even forgot to pick up some lunch so head to McDonald's on the way back. I am never going to be a size 10 again.

18.30

I get home from what feels like another tiring day at work, pick up the post from the letter box, throw my bag down on the floor and grab my phone to watch the video of how to do the Haka.

I remember we had a substitute teacher from New Zealand when I was about eight years old and he taught us the Haka in a music lesson but I can't remember any of the moves. So here goes.

19.00

This is so fun! I have mastered it and filmed myself to send to my Nan.

When Jack comes in, I am sitting on the sofa watching 'Don't tell the Bride' On this episode the groom is arranging a wedding on an ice rink. This would be my worst nightmare. Even though I haven't thought about marriage yet, people say it's meant to be the best day of your life and, for it to be the best day of MY life, it would need to be hot. The best day of my life will not include ice unless it's in a Pina colada!

I can hear Jack's keys coming in the door and I remember I can't speak to him for an hour.

'Smizzel!' He says excitedly (he sometimes calls me that because my surname is Smith so it's just a nickname).

I look up to acknowledge he is there but I don't reply.

'You alright?' He suddenly panics dropping his rucksack on the floor. Probably because the drama I caused yesterday about Kathy. Damn this was not a good day to do this.

But I just nod and carry on watching TV.

He sits up close to me and puts his arm around my shoulders. The cold from his jacket makes me squirm and I move away quickly. 'What's up? Are you ok?'

All of a sudden, a wave of guilt comes over me. I have made him worry and I can't explain that I'm fine and that I have only been told by Regina that I can't talk to him.

I look up at him but then look back to the TV.

'What's up?' Now he sounds frustrated. 'Is it me? Is it work? What is it? Just tell me.'

I carry on watching TV but this has to stop soon so I look at my phone and its only 19.12pm. Oh God! I have 48 minutes left!

He has had enough. 'Ok fine.' He snaps. 'Well tell me when you want to talk' and he walks off into the kitchen, pours himself a glass of water and leaves the room. I'm not sure why, as we don't have a TV in the bedroom but I suppose he just wants to get away from me.

By this time, the bride has now seen her dress and HATES it! To be fair it's not that bad but it comes with a long train and he has chosen 6-inch stilettos. I mean, I hope he has hired an ambulance as well. This wedding this look dangerous. I love it when they get it wrong, I know it sounds bitchy but it's funny and surely that's the point of the show.

I'm intrigued to know what Jack is doing so I go into the bedroom to 'get some clothes for a wash'. He has his headphones on watching something on his phone.

He doesn't acknowledge I'm there but doesn't seem too pissed off either. He's too engrossed in whatever he is watching (probably football). As I head towards the door, he takes a headphone out, 'Elise, are you ok?'

Shit! I feel so bad. But not that bad because I carry on walking. I'm not sure why I went in there now, I have made it look so much worse.

I start to make dinner because, then, when I do finally talk to him, maybe that will soften the blow if he's annoyed. I got mince out this morning so I'm going to make fajitas. I know most people make it with chicken but I prefer it with mince.

20.00

We are sitting opposite each other in silence eating fajitas WITH NO FUCKING CHEESE! I should have gone back to get some cheese.

10

9

8

7

6

5

4

3

2

1

'Right, now I can explain. Regina wrote me a list and one of the things on it was not to speak to you for an hour.' I breath out, as if I have been holding my breath.

'Ok,' he grunts.

Oh shit, he's pissed off!

'Sorry I know I should have written it down, just want to do these lists properly and then it will make them more exciting.'

'I don't know how not talking is *exciting*.' He air-quotes the word 'exciting'.

'I know but it's just what was on my list.'

'Are you going to do this every night?' he asks. 'A list every day?'

Woah, he seems really pissed off and a little hurt.

'I quite like it and I'm doing different things and it's fun! Why don't you write me a list?'

'Oh, I don't know what to put on a list,' he snaps.

'Anything. It's just 5 things for me to do within a 24-hour period, it will be fun.'

'I'm rubbish at things like that.'

'List 5 things you want me to do then. It doesn't have to be fun things or doesn't have to be life changing, just little tasks. It could be football related or a job you want me to do around the flat, just anything.'

'I'll have a think,' he smiles and taps my knee as if to apologise for being grumpy.

'Do it! I will do yours tomorrow.' I'm quite excited.

'OK,' he agrees.

'Let's go pub and cheer ourselves up.'

'Ok, but you're buying the first round.'

'Deal!'

22.00

We weren't out long but after a quick pint it's all forgotten and we had a really good night. I told him all about today's list and the drama of the dress – I mean I did text him when I was being taken to hospital but was updating him on the details.

'Oh Jack!' I shout from the kitchen. 'There's some post for you on the coffee table,' and I carry on making myself some toast. I always fancy toast after a drink.

'There's one addressed to you. It looks quite official,' he says and he hands me the letter. I look at him confused because post never arrives for me, I opted for paperless banking and it's not like people write letters these days. I open the letter and it's from the NS&I:

Dear Miss Smith,

CONGRATULATIONS! You have won £25 in our monthly draw.

No way! I won £25 from my premium bonds! Already? That's crazy! I squeal and run to jack flapping the letter all over place.

'Jack! Look! I won!' I'm on such high and jumping around.

'Won what?' He is laughing because I'm like a hysterical child.

'A few weeks ago, I bought £500 worth of Premium Bonds and I won £25!'

'Wow really? That's amazing! How did you do that? Can I buy them?' He grabs the iPad and starts looking it up.

'Yeah course, anyone can, I'm so excited! I didn't think I would win anything! Especially not that quick!'

'That is pretty cool I'm going to do it now then we have double the chance of winning big!'

'It says here that I can invest the £25 back in and buy more bonds,' I am reading the letter to him.

'Yeah, do that then we can keep investing! Well done girl!' He says and kisses my cheek.

I smile and strut off the kitchen to pick up my cold toast.

Well this evening ended better than it started. I wonder what he will put on my list? Probably cook him steak and iron his shirts. Actually, do we even own an iron?

Well we'll see tomorrow. He has been writing something in his notepad since we got in so this should be interesting.

Chapter 6 – Word starts to spread

25th January

06.26

'Jack?' I whisper. 'Did, you write me a list? I will do it today.'

His alarm hasn't gone off yet but he must be awake because mine has been going off every 10 minutes for the past half an hour.

'Jack!' I push his shoulder.

'What?' he grunts.

'Did you write me a list? I'm going to work and I will do it today.'

'Oh no. Sorry I forgot. I'll write it today.'

'Oh, ok cool, no worries. Just put anything on there and I will do it tomorrow.'

So, I'm list free today but that suits because I'm going out with Regina later. Well, Regina minus Zee because she's ill.

08.03

I get to work on time which means Kathy is in a good mood!

'Morning Elise! You alright?' she chirps.

I sit down slowly as I'm not sure how to handle this change.

'Yes, great thanks, how about you?' I ask, nervously.

'Great, thank you, how was your evening?' She carries on, still looking at me and still seeming interested.

'Erm, yeah, good actually. Well, last night was a bit weird actually because…' I stop because I realise she would not be interested in this at all. It was only a follow up question, but when I looked up, she was still looking at me as if she was waiting for the story. Do I tell her about last night?

I hesitate for a minute, then like verbal diarrhoea the whole story of List Life comes out.

'I have been doing this thing for the last couple of days where people have been giving me a list of tasks to complete in 24 hours. It can be anything as long as I can complete them within a 24-hour period, so it can't be travel around the world or only eat cheese for a week. But anything that is achievable within a day.'

Bill pipes up, 'How about not talk for a whole day!' He half laughs and looks very proud of himself. Well, technically that would be a good one and does actually count but I ignore him because he's being a prick.

I carry on, 'So yeah, yesterday I couldn't swear all day and had to not speak to Jack for an hour when he came in, which didn't go down too well but we are ok now.'

Kathy laughed, which I have never seen her do before well, not at my jokes. We start talking about all the things I have done, like bake a cake and stroke a dog and been to see Lala Land.

'Can I do you one then?' she asks. Oh, wow, I was not expecting that!

'Yes! Of course! It will be fun.' I screech.

'Ok give me until after lunch and I will write you a list.'

'Ok great!' This was exciting! She never normally ever even talks to me, especially in the morning AND she thinks it's a great idea. Winner already!

13.35

It's lunch time and we are heading to this deli bar I saw the other day and have been thinking about ever since.

'So, Kathy is going to write you a list?' Brad is confused.

'Yep!' I'm smiling and bursting with success. I told him the whole story as soon as we jumped in the car.

'But what will she put on it? She knows nothing about you?' He seems a bit pissed off but I ignore it as I'm too excited.

'No idea but it will be interesting to know, won't it?

'Not really. I bet she stitches you up. Why is she even getting involved?'

'Alright Brad! Calm down!' He's in a right mood. 'I told her about List Life and she said she wanted to join in. Let me just enjoy the moment. She likes me for once.'

'Fair enough, just didn't think you cared that much about her liking you.' he mumbles whilst looking out the passenger window.

Oh jeeez! Why's he getting all funny about it. Men are weird.

I park up and we go and get some food. Maybe he's just hungry.

14.33

When I get back to the office, Tom is looking all smug and nodding over at Kathy.

I turn to Kathy, who is looking so proud of herself and says 'Here it is,' as she passes me a folded post-it-note.

'Great! Thank you!' I match her excitement.

As I read the list out loud, she, Tom and Bill are all staring at me smiling.

'Listen to a radio News channel on the way to work.' (Oh, jeez these people are so boring)

'Watch sport with Jack when you get in.

Don't go out for lunch with Brad, stay in the staff room.' (Clever).

'Cook a three-course meal.'

Oh God! Brad was right and he's going to be fuming about the lunch one. Ok, well this works out well anyway because Brad isn't in tomorrow so HA! Nice try. Also, I know I have pissed Jack off so a three-course meal will be a great way of making it up to him.

'No worries guys I can do this, it will start at midnight tonight.'

Bill is staring at me over the desk with such a smug look on his face. 'You hate the News don't you Elise?'

I roll my eyes. 'Yes Bill, I do, but one day can't hurt.' Ok, so this is what makes him happy, making my life hell. Fair enough.

Kathy and Tom have been buzzing all afternoon and telling everyone about the list they have created for me. Steve thinks it's 'Unbelievable'. No shit.

18.30

I get a text from Dawn saying she can't make tonight either so it's just me and Rosie. Even she is debating meeting up now without the others.

Rosie you have to come, I owe you £4.20 from yesterday.

Oh Jeez! How much to do you swear?

Do you want it or not? I text, whilst rolling my eyes.

Ok, sure, that can buy my dessert.

21.45

Even though she's a little whiner, I like going out with Rosie! She's very pretty and all the guys love her, BUT she has terrible taste in men! As I mentioned before she has been dating for a few months now but she hasn't met anyone she really likes. In all honestly, she is still hung up on her ex. So, I will quickly tell you the story:

She met him on a night out (it was a work night out but he didn't work with us). They spent the night together and then, against all dating theories, they actually ended up together. He claimed he had a son with another woman but they had separated on bad terms so no one could find out that they were together. Obviously, she fell for this utter bullshit and carried on as normal. He has never taken her out anywhere within a 10-mile radius of the town they live in and he takes her on lavish holidays with the understanding that she is not allowed to post any photos of them together in case they get caught by this 'big bad' ex-girlfriend.

So, one day my sister, Ava was showing me photos of a night out she had with friends and I saw Kevin (the man in question) with a blonde girl. I asked who it was and she said it was her mate Rachel's fiancé. FIANCE?! I was shocked, not only did he have a girlfriend they were planning a wedding!

So, I spoke to Dawn, to see what she thought and obviously we decided to tell Rosie, which was awful because she was heartbroken. She confronted him that night and he told her that they had split up and that they put on a front to other people for the sake of the kid.

ANYWAY! This was about a year and a half ago and it's all still going on. He lies, she believes him, he lies again, she doesn't believe him, they row, they split up, they get back together! Oh!

The drama just keeps going.

Tonight, the drama is that she messaged the girlfriend and the girl had no idea and had flipped out at her and Kevin, which has now resulted in all of them splitting up! But this could change as he will no doubt lie again.

Anyway, I gave Rosie the money and she brought a fudge brownie and I had cheese cake.

We have asked for the bill and I am telling her about not talking to Jack and how it didn't go down to well.

'Oh yeah me and Kevin used to do that all the time,' she says and looks down at the table. Oh God I need to change the subject hmm…. just in time the waitress returns with the bill.

'Can I just say you are so pretty. My colleague and I were just saying how stunning you are,' she blurts out.

She is staring at Rosie by the way, not me, not that you needed that explaining. This is so awkward. What am I meant to do in this situation? I just sip my lime and soda and look around the room.

'Oh, thank you,' Rosie nervously laughs and picks up the bill. The waitress was obviously feeling no embarrassment as she carries on:

'Are your lashes real? If not, where do you get them done?'

'Erm yes. Yes, they are real.' Rosie coughs, then looks at me as if urging me to say something.

'Can you tell me where the toilets are please?' I ask because I need to get out of here, it's so cringe.

‘Over there’ the creep responds and points in the direction of the ladies.

‘Thanks!’ I jump up and leave Rosie to get rid of her. Rosie raises her eyebrows at me with wide eyes but I ignore her.

I wait in the toilets for about 5 minutes, messing around with my hair, topping up my lippy, then grab my phone: *Has she gone yet?*

Yes! Now get out here will you, I can’t believe you left me with her!

I get back to the table and she is standing there with her coat on and we just couldn’t control our laughter. ‘Where’s your date?’ I joke.

‘Shut up! Come on let’s get out of here.’

22.30

When I get home, Jack is watching football (obviously). Well he’s watching the highlights from the game he has only just watched.

I tell him all about Rosie’s drama and he seems pretty invested. He’s never met Kevin but says he isn’t surprised and thinks they will get back together.

‘Anyway more importantly, have you written me a list?’ I ask.

‘Sorry Elise, I was watching the game and I don’t know what to put on it.’

'Jack!' I moan. 'It's nothing serious. It's just a list of things to do throughout the day. What would you like me to do?'

'I don't know.'

'Ok well, have a think and let me know. Kathy has written me one to do tomorrow anyway, so I will do yours another day.'

'KATHY!? As in your boss Kathy?'

'Yep!'

'Oh God! What does that say? Stay away from Brad?'

'To be fair one of them is to not have lunch with him tomorrow.' We both laugh.

'She's crazy… maybe she fancies him.'

'It's a possibility. Anyway, I'm going to go to bed to read.'

'Alright you little bookworm, I'll be in soon.'

I haven't read my 'Yes Man' book in a while so I'll read that.

Night guys x

25th January

07.05

'O*n 17 January 2017 the* Prime Minister set out the 12 principles *which will guide the government in fulfilling the democratic will of the people of the United Kingdom. In this White Paper the government sets out the basis for these priorities and the approach to forging a new strategic partnership between the United Kingdom and the EU.'*

Do people actually listen to this? People are actually calling the radio station to rant and rave about the government. Who is this angry about the government? And who is this angry at 7.15 in the morning?

The traffic starts to slow.

'And now time for the traffic news – There are currently delays of up to 45-minute heading anti-clockwise on M25 between junction 24-22, due to an overturned vehicle.'

Oh lord! An extra 45 minutes of this station. Well at least I lose 45 minutes of being at work. Hope the people involved in the accident are ok.

09.05

When I get to work Bill is the only one in (Maybe they are all stuck in that traffic). His face lights up as soon as he sees me (first time for everything).

'So? Did you listen to the News?' he bursts as if he has been thinking about that all night and is ready to test me.

'Yes of course, it's List Life. They were raving on about a piece of paper!' I switch my computer on and try not to make eye-contact because I am bored of the News now – two hours is way too much.

He laughed (which I've never seen him do). 'The White paper?'

'Erm, possibly, I don't know what colour it was?'

He's laughing hysterically now. But I am very confused. It didn't seem that funny when they were talking about it.

'Yes, it's called 'The White Paper' he explains, but I am really not that bothered 'It's a Government report giving information or proposals on an issue.'

'Ohh, makes sense now.'

And then it dawned on me Bill is talking to me and he's getting excited about something, which is kind of cool, even if it is the most boring subject in the world. I let him ramble on and nod in the right places.

09.30

Finally, Kathy and Tom arrive! I am not normally excited to see them but Bill is driving me mad now and he won't stop.

'Hi Tom!' I jump up. 'Shall we go and make some tea. Kathy do you want a cuppa?'

'Yeah! Sure, thanks Elise! Be careful this time though.' She laughs. 'Have you done any of the list I gave you?'

I laugh too but trying so hard to make it sound sarcastic. 'Yep! I'll just get a drink and then I'll tell you about my drive in.' I head off to the kitchen and can hear Bill explaining it to Kathy anyway. Thank god.

When we return with the drinks (And some biscuits I found the cupboard) I sit down and tell them about the News. They are shocked and excited that I done it. They said they didn't think I would do it. Kathy said she listens to that channel every morning. Well that explains a lot!

12.45

As Kathy is in a weirdly, good mood, I take the opportunity to text Brad without having to hide my phone under the desk: *Oh God I am dreading lunch! I have to spend it in this building, which means I'm not leaving here until the end of the day.*

You asked Kathy, what did you expect?

They are being ok today so it might be fun.

Ahaha…maybe.

Yeah. I know he's right. It's going to be hell. He's been a bit funny with me about this list and I'm not sure why it's upset him so much. I understand she has been a Bitch and now all of a sudden she's playing along as if we are best friends but who cares. What if this changes our relationship? Surely that's a good thing.

They want to go on lunch at 1pm so that works, it's not too early. Only 15 more minutes.

13.25

You know sometimes when you think something is going to be horrendous and then it turns out not quite as bad you think it's going to be? Well this wasn't one of them!

A few things about this joke of a lunch:

- I have to stay in this building, which is so depressing. It's not like we have a really cool canteen. It's just a spare room with a big table and a vending machine.
- We went on our lunch 'hour' and they all decided they needed to get back after 25 minutes.
- Bill talked about lawn mowers THE WHOLE TIME, he's not even a gardener!
- Kathy was on her phone to her husband and ignored me.
- Last but not least, I had pizza while they were all eating salad (actually that might be a win).

And THAT'S why I go out at lunch! The News, then this. Seriously, is this what they do with their lives? They need a list but I very much doubt I could get any of this lot to do one. Tom didn't come on lunch with us because he said he needed a spiritual energy re-charge. Well so do I now! I feel like my soul has fucked off.

17.15

The rest of the afternoon was painful and silent. I have spent the majority of the time messaging Brad and Regina, which I shouldn't have been doing I know, but today Kathy was my only friend and seemed to be asking a lot about the lists. She thought the one about the dog and Adele was hilarious! Course she did, it was a stitch up. Right I need to sort myself out she was actually being nice today and I need to not be a bitch.

I will go and make us all tea.

19.15

When Jack gets in, he thinks he has won the lottery!

'Oh, hello sir, come in take a seat.' I point to the table that I have set up (I don't have candles, because let's be honest, would you trust me with a naked flame?)

'What's all this about?' He looks nervous.

'Can't a woman cook her man a nice meal without a reason?' I attempt to say in a seductive voice.

'Was it on your list?' he asks bluntly.

'Well yeah, but it's still cool right?' sounding more like a cockney from the East End.

Tonight's Menu is:

Prawn cocktail to start

Salmon and sweet potato wedges for the main

Pomelo and ice-cream for dessert (because I had loads of it left over).

It was surprisingly delicious! Once we had finished my 'fine dining' experience, we sit down and watch cricket because he said there wasn't any football on. It is actually a really good evening in the end. We had a few beers and he explained the rules of the game. You learn something new every day.

I didn't ask if he had done a list because it was clear he hadn't and I didn't want to ruin the night. He clearly wasn't bothered about it or maybe he thought it was a stupid idea.

Surprisingly, despite the fact I think she wanted to challenge me, Kathy's list was actually quite fun, apart from the lunch. That was awful!

26th January

18.30

It's Friday so I am going for a drink with Brad as promised. We are meeting at the pub because we live in different directions so it makes no sense going together after work as we would have to come back to work to pick our cars up. Like I said, I have never been out with Brad outside of work because I see him all day.

We sit down and order two gourmet beef burgers, a pint of San Miguel and a Carlsberg. (I know, I know, I am on a diet, but it's Friday).

First, we start a full-on bitch sesh about Kathy and Bill because they were not in the same mood as yesterday. Kathy was in a right strop today. Luckily for me she had a few meetings so wasn't about much.

He then goes on to tell me that his friend lives in Dubai and wants him to go over for a visit but he doesn't know if he should go there or use the money to go on holiday to a country he has never been to before.

'Have you been to India?' I ask because he seems like the type of guy that would love India.

'No, I haven't actually but I just think it's not the type of place I should be going on my own, I've heard horror stories about solo travelers getting themselves into all sorts of situations.'

I get a buzz of excitement through my spine because I am just about to rave on about my trip to India.

'You can do a tour!!' I suggest. 'A few years ago, Jack and I went to India and did an eight-day tour of the Golden Triangle. It was so cool! We went to Delhi, Agra, Japiur! You get to see the Taj Mahal, visit the markets, ride camels and watch Bollywood movies, it was AMAZING!'

'Hmmm, I'm not too sure. Was it one of those 18-30's trips where…?'

'Nope!' I interrupt. 'It was a mixed group. There was a couple the same age as us from Canada, two elderly ladies who said the Taj Mahal was on their bucket list, a middle age couple who came over to attend their daughter's wedding and then did the tour afterwards and a girl on her own who had split up with her boyfriend, so needed an adventure.. maybe you should look into it.' But before he could argue with me anymore, I write down the name of the tour company's website and change the conversation to one about food…obviously.

21.00

It turned out to be a really good night. We chatted about the countries we had travelled to, a bit more about the crazy people at work and then about List life.

He admitted that he was a bit annoyed about the list Kathy gave me and he was a bit annoyed with me for asking her for one as she had been so bitchy towards me before.

'The lists are meant to be a way of cheering someone up or being productive.'

'Yeah, I know but that's how I see them too, but technically it did make me do new stuff and build a good relationship with her, even if it was for only one day.'

'True but it shouldn't start to be a way of making someone unhappy.'

'Calm down, it was only a laugh.' I find myself defending her.

'I know just don't want to ruin it, anyway it's your round' and he points towards the bar.

22.00

We are just putting our coats on and getting ready to leave, when

I see a petite blonde lady approaching us, accompanied by a tall Italian looking guy, wearing one of those long, arrogant jackets.

'Brad?' She asks in a 'trying too hard' posh accent.

Brad obviously recognises the voice and mouths 'Oh shit!' to me.

As he turns around, he screeches, 'Amanda! Fancy seeing you here!'

'Hi! I thought it was you and didn't know whether to come over,' she says nervously.

I don't know who this woman is but it all feels very awkward. Mr 'long jacket' is standing a few meters away and is glancing around the room as if he's on the lookout.

'How have you been?' Brad asks. He sounds nervous.

'Yeah, fine just popped out for a drink after work with ermm….so how's things? What you been up to?' She quickly changes the subject.

I am so confused. Maybe it's an old friend? A girlfriend? OH SHIT! It's just clicked. THE EX WIFE!

I stand close to him just for reassurance but she whips her head round and looks me up and down. To be fair she seems just as nervous as him.

'Erm, oh this and that, we were just…' He hesitates and looks at me. I smile as if to say 'you got this'. Then he stands up tall and looks her in the eye and out of nowhere 'We were just talking about my trip to India.' Woah!

'India?' She looks surprised.

'Yeah, I'm going there on one of those backpacking tours to visit the Golden Triangle,' he carries on.

Yes Brad! You are smashing it! I can't help my ridiculous grin.

'Wow that sounds amazing! You're really living life to the full aren't you.' She looks quite jealous.

'Yeah, I've wanted to do it for a while now and thought this is the perfect time.'

'Well I'll let you get on and erm…have fun in India.' She waves, hooks arms with the Italian spy and off she goes.

I really want to do my happy dance but Brad knows what I'm thinking and shakes he's head at me. When the coast is clear we head to the car park.

'Wow, that was amazing! So, are you actually going to India?' I am buzzing!

'Well I'm going to have to now, aren't I? We know the same people so they will tell her if I don't!'

'Woo, you are going to love it!' I clap my hands together and grin like a Cheshire cat.

He is shaking his head at me but seems to be finding it funny. 'Why do I listen to you?'

'Because I'm a genius.'

27th January

12.00

Today is SATURDAY! It's Will's Dads 60th birthday party and I've agreed to help him decorate the hall.

I have known Will since being at school, and we have a love/hate relationship. Most of the time I want to throw him off a cliff but then catch him at the bottom. I thought he was so hot at school, probably because he paid me attention and he was the only one that did so it felt nice. When we left school, it turned out he was gay, which made sense really. He is still quite hot though. We have been best friends ever since.

I walk to the party shop up the road and grab balloons, party poppers and a banner. All requested by Will. I'm not sure why he isn't doing this, it's his Dad, but I have loads of time today so don't mind helping out.

Jack has popped into town to get a shirt for the occasion and I've asked him to pick me up a pair of tights to go with my purple velvet dress.

16.30

I arrive at the community hall, park up and wander in. It's a massive hall, high ceilings and has a stage with thick red curtains. There doesn't seem to be anyone around.

'Hello?' I call out.

Will pops his head out from the kitchen. 'Oh, thank God! I thought you bailed on me! Did you get everything?'

'Yep! All here, I didn't know if you wanted Blue and White for

Chelsea or Red for Saracens?'

'Oh, either. He's obsessed with both.'

'Ok good I went for blue and white.' I boast, feeling all proud of myself.

'Good, come on! We have loads to do!' He snaps.

Oh, good God. He's so bossy but I do as I'm told and crack on.

19.00

Guests are due to arrive any minute and I am getting changed in the toilets in a rush. I am in a panic because Jack has bought fishnets instead of sheer black tights. Well this is *so* inappropriate for my friend's, Dad's 60th birthday party. It's going to look like they have hired adult entertainment.

I can hear guests arriving and Will apologising for me not being there to hand out glasses of fizz, so I rush out and help. As he sees me her gasps.

'*What* are you wearing?!' He flings his hands up to his head.

'Is it really that bad?'

'Yes, he's going to think we have ordered him a lap dance, just go bare legged!' He looks so stressed and sends me back to the toilets. Wow this guy is aggy today, but I do as I'm told.

21.45

Finally, I can grab a drink. He has had me working all evening and I'm so thirsty.

'Alright trouble?' Will's Dad finally gets to the bar and I ask him what he is having.

'No worries love, Will should be getting them in. I heard you helped my boys do all this so, thank you. I really appreciate it.'

I nudge him with my elbow and scrunch my face up. 'Don't go all soft on me now Des.'

'You were always an 'ard nut to crack. Where's your fella anyway? I haven't seen him yet tonight and I want to wind him up about the score the other night,' He turns away with his pint and finds Jack.

I order a vodka and coke and a pint and head off to find Will. He is sitting on a chair looking out on the party. 'What's up?' I ask as I pass him his drink.

'Nothing, just look at everyone having fun. It's a great night and Dad was so surprised. We smashed it, didn't we?' And he holds up a hand for me to high five.

'We really did. Are you staying for the weekend or heading home tomorrow?'

'Heading home. I have to work Monday and I've got a meeting to prepare for.'

'Oo, Mr Importante' (practicing my Spanish at any given moment)

He shakes his head. He hates it when I tease him about his high-flying job. But I'm not lying, he has smashed it in the working world. We went to school together and he left without any grades,

(Do English people call it grades or is that American?) he then went and worked in a shop, got promoted to manager then worked on an airline, travelled the world and now works in a high-end London store getting paid the big bucks. I went on to A'levels, a degree, travelled and am still poor and unsuccessful. Lesson learnt: do what you want to in life because you will succeed if you are happy. By the way I am happy…just thought it was a chance to add a bit of wisdom.

'I might do the London Marathon this year,' he announces, randomly.

'Can you run?' I know for sure I can't.

'No, but I couldn't walk once but you just gotta practice.'

'Actually, that's true,' I laugh. 'Hey, remember that time we were on the flight to Kavos and you were gripping onto my arm, sweating about the take off and then the next year told me you got a job as an air steward.'

'Exactly, fear will get you nowhere. Now let's go and do a shot of Tequila with the birthday boy because I *fear* he's not drunk enough to be talking to Aunty Sarah!'

01.30

It's been a great night, Des is amazing. I think he had a few too many shots in the end because he got emotional when making a speech. Will and I did our best to take the mick after but we were just as drunk.

Jack is getting all soppy in the taxi back and starts telling me how he loves 'us' and that every day is like an adventure. I thought this was chance to get him to write a list but as soon as we get home, we both pass out on the sofa.

28th January

As expected, I am VERY hungover.

Three in one coffee and a fry up down the café, I think. Jack doesn't need persuading and is first out the door.

'Two full English's, one coffee, one tea and two orange juices please,' I order. The lady serving us looks like she needs the same. I am over the days when I have to work hungover. I once went to work feeling awful and I worked in a bar at the time. My boss made me clean the cigarette butts from the beer garden patio with a pair of tweezers on the hottest day of the year. I mean what a punishment. Cruel man. I'd like to say it taught me a lesson, but it didn't. I turned up hungover to work every Saturday when I was 18.

11.00

Back at the flat and I have written myself 'hangover cure' list:

Have a refreshing shower using all shower products

Drink eight glasses of water

Go for a long walk in the woods

Eat everything in sight

Do the 'I'm a dreamer' routine

I will start with glass of water number one and then jump in the shower.

15.15

This has gone horribly wrong. I am in the middle of the woods and I am desperate for the toilet. Drinking four glasses of water before I came out was not a good idea. Jack seems to know where we are and says there is a pub about ten minutes away. What is it with men? How do they just know where they are in the middle of trees? My Dad is exactly the same.

I can see the pub now and am walking as fast as I can and occasionally shouting back at Jack 'COME ON! I am going to pee myself!'

'I'm coming! You know where it is now, we don't have to both run. I will meet you outside.'

I leg it to the pub and burst through the door causing a scene.

'Could I please use your toilet?' I beg.

'Yes, but you will need to purchase a drink first,' she says through pursed lips and still towel drying the wine glasses. WHAT?! How does that make sense? That would make it worse. Now I have to wait for Jack because he has the money. I am bouncing from one foot to the other, biting my fist. I don't care how crazy I look, she knows the situation.

Jack strolls in the pub and buys us both a lime soda and I run to the toilet.

I made it thank god.

I'm back to the table now and I'm quite glad we stopped for a drink. I've never been to this pub before but we can't have walked too far. I have an idea.

'I was writing a list this morning and one of them was to do my 'I'm a dreamer' routine, do you want to do it with me in the field, over road once we have finished these drinks?' (Don't be rude, I mean the I'm a dreamer routine)

'Well I can't let you do it on your own, can I? And, now you have got it in your head this is happening,' he laughs.

'Woo thank you; we don't have shades but we could ask for a bottle of water to take with us as our drink.'

'Yeah, I'll go grab a couple now, make sure you go to the toilet before we go, you're like a sieve.' and he heads of to the bar. I take his advice and pop to the loo.

16.20

We are laying on our coats in a secluded field and blasting 'I'm a Dreamer' from my phone. It's not quite the beach vibe I normally go for but it's fun! Yet again, Jack is joining in without any questions. He has his eyes closed and seems to be quite chilled. I am chilled – I'm flipping freezing! But it does make me calm and refreshed. When the song ends, we jump up brush off the grass and head back the way we came.

18.05

Neither of us can be bothered to cook tonight but I am so hungry and we decide to walk up the road to treat ourselves to an all-you-can-eat carvery. I only have water to drink, which works out well because I refill the glass 3 times and it's free.

Even though it wasn't exactly the list life rules, I did write myself one and it was fun and I feel much better than this morning, so it worked.

I am so hyped up, that when I get in, I text my pals for a list for tomorrow. I'm a little bit addicted now.

Chapter 7 – Which type of friend are you?

29th January

Tonight, Jack is at football, as per usual and my pals have given me a list which consists of:

Give yourself a landing strip! (obviously Tanya gave that one! I'll introduce Tanya later).

Learn to say 'Hello my name is Elise and I'm Ginger' in Spanish

All items of clothing you wear today have to be different colours

Eat two - 12inch pizzas

Text all your pals telling them why you love them (They just want me to suck up to them)

06.45

My alarm didn't go off and I woke up 15 minutes late, so now I only five minutes to get ready and out! First, I start with a purple bra and a bright pink pair of knickers. Class! Next, I find some red jeans and pray they still fit, fling on a yellow t-shirt and now for shoes hmmm silver pumps. DONE…gross but easy! But I am 20 minutes late leaving.

08.15

'Morning Ronald McDonald' Brad laughs as I walk in.

'Eh? Oh, the outfit Ha! All my items of clothes have to be different colours.'

'Couldn't you just choose blue jeans and black boots, like you normally do?'

'Well, yes, I could have but I didn't think of that, plus this is way more fun!'

'I'm sure Kathy will think it's 'fun'

Yeah that might be a problem.

10.30

I'm so bored! Tom told me that him and his boyfriend have split up but they will probably see each other again because he was married to him in his previous life and in the life before that they owned a horse and cart business together. HELP ME!

Kathy hasn't spoken to me all morning which is driving me mad. Who acts like that as a boss? Maybe I should flirt outrageously with Brad and she might talk to me to get the goss.

12.45

Oh god I feel bad now! Kathy had to rush off because she got a call to say that her son was in a fight at school and he seems to be hurt. I can't imagine Kathy as a Mum. She's only 32, so quite young. She doesn't seem like the soft type who would tuck you in at night and read a bedtime story. I mean she doesn't talk about them a lot but has a photo on her desk of her husband Stuart and three children – two boys, one girl. Anyway, hopefully he is ok and it was just a playground scuffle. It does mean however, that I have been left with all the invoices from last week.

13.30

As per usual Brad is being dragged round the supermarket. I need to buy two large pizzas. Tanya is fun, flirty and always up for a laugh. When I was about 16, I used to go to hers and we would go on MSN, this online chat thing, and talk to guys just for a laugh really. Obviously, the guys were our age so it wasn't anything dodgy. We would buy the cheapest, supermarket pizzas and a bottle of coke. So that's the pizza I chose today, for old times' sake, and the second one was a chicken, pepper, sweetcorn with bbq sauce. I'm quite a big eater so I think this will be easy.

16.30

Brad texts me even though we sit opposite each other because stroppy knickers doesn't like us talking so we have to email or text. I don't think she's coming back in this afternoon so not sure why he still does it.

Saturday is Chinese New Year. We should celebrate!

Yess!! Let's do this! What do they do?

I will find out what the traditions are and let you know.

Perfecto!

18.30

Finally, home! Traffic was disgusting and I'm starving. I've put the pizzas in the oven and going to jump in the shower. Tonight, I'm having a proper girly night on my own while Jack is out.

18.45

Attempted a landing strip but was a bit difficult as I waxed last night. Not sure how I will prove that one but they will have to take my word for it. Dressing gown, face mask and wine…I know it's Monday but who cares. It's only 5 days until the weekend. I think I'm going to watch 'What women want' a proper chick flick. Ahh bliss!

19.45

One pizza down, that was easy! Right now, to be a drip to my mates I will start with Molly.

I *love that you accept anything I do and don't question me.*

Text Will – *I love our nights out and that you always do shots with me.*

Text Natalie – *Best pal to gossip with over a glass of wine.*

Text Brad - *I love that you join in with my ideas like List Life*

Text Tanya - *I love that you are so clumsy it takes the spot light off my stupidity*

Text Graham - *I couldn't live without you, you are always there to save the day*

Text Jack - *I love you*

22.00

The next pizza starts off easy, bit more flavour and nicely washed down with my wine. It's been sliced into 8 slices so that I can have a break at any point.

Mel Gibson seems to be having a girlier night than me with all these products he is experimenting with. Men have it easy. They don't have to wax or get their eyebrows done. Then, when you mention this to them, they say 'I like the naturelle look'…Yeah course you do mate. That's why you chatted me up when I was wearing a full face of makeup, hair extensions and lashes I could take off and dust the table with.

5 slices down and I am really struggling.

I get up and start pacing the room and stretching! Never knew eating pizza could feel like an olympic sport. I stand in the middle of the room with my hand on my hips and look up at the ceiling COME ON ELISE!! You can do this!!!

I carry on eating but standing up because I feel sick.

Oh my god, I'm so full! I have one more slice and it's painful. This looked so easy. Right 1, 2, 3 go! And I demolish the last slice! Oh my god, I'm going to throw up! 2 pizzas and ¾ of a bottle of wine. This was not a good idea! As I mentioned wine is not my friend but it was all I had in the flat.

22.45

Laying on the bathroom floor and been heaving every 5 minutes. I can hear my phone buzzing in the living room. I need to get up and stop being dramatic.

23.03

Laying on the sofa feeling sorry for myself and the weirdest thing has happened! Brad just text me saying he has Googled traditions of Chinese New Year and one of them is *Eating Pomelos*. That is the freakiest thing ever! He sent me this (obviously copied from Google):

Eating Pomelos is thought to bring continuous prosperity. The more you eat the more wealth it will bring.

This is crazy! It's like fate. I didn't even know what one was the other day now I have one in my fridge. I am going to buy another one for Saturday. I need more to make me rich! Super Yacht I am coming for ya!

Right going to bed, oh and by the way 'Hola mi nombre es Elise y soy jengibre'

Smashed it. Peace out!

30th January

08.15

Who is that sitting at my desk?

Tom seems to be in deep conversation with her but she doesn't look like she's listening. Kathy is in a shirt and suit jacket. Hmm, what's going on?

'Hi?' I try not to sound rude, but who is she?

'Hi!' Tom chirps. The girl doesn't even look up from MY desk. I look at Kathy and shrug.

'Hi Elise, this is Monica. She is joining our team. You did get a company email.'

A company email? Ok, for a start yes, I should have read the company email but why didn't Kathy just tell me face to face. Oh, why am I bothering?

'Hi Monica, hows it going?' I ask because maybe this is my chance to make a friend here.

'Fine, thank you.' She doesnt look up, but nods. She has an accent but I'm not sure where it's from.

Kathy is in her element, rearranging desks to seat me in between the wizard and my silent friend.

'Elise, will get you set up on the system Monica and then, at 12.30pm, I'll take you over the road for a bit of lunch. Does that sounds good?'

Sound good? Of course it sounds good FOR YOU! Now I have to make small talk, teach a job I don't know very well myself, then get ditched for lunch! Sod it, lets just get on with this.

'So, first we need to set you up on the system,' I start typing 'Monica' into the profile section. 'It's Monica with a K' she murmers but doesn't take her eyes away from the screen.

'Ok no worries,' I chirp and carry on. 'So where were you working before?'

'For an investent company in central.' Still no eye contact.

'Oh, this is a bit different then, what made you change?'

She just shrugged. Wow this is hard.

I set her up and take her through some of the bits I dont like doing, then let her get on with that for the day. Everyones got to start somewhere right?

12.35

Finally, they have gone on lunch. That morning dragged. Now I can chill until my lunch break.

I grab my phone open up Facebook and scroll through the baby photos with the caption 'Think we have an artist in the making', the before and after photos of random women who have lost 10lbs in 4 hours on the latest diet and endless memes letting us know that 'that she's come to her senses and she does not need a man'. I click 'Like' on all of them because I do actually like them. I like the fact that they all have a little faith.

13.45

'Who's your new mate?' Brad asks as soon as we get in the car 'She's hot!'

'Maybe she'll talk to you. I can't get a word out of her.'

'Use the Brad charm,' he winks.

I roll my eyes and start the engine.

14.05

We grab a sandwich meal deal from the shop and sit in the car park chatting, about our morning.

'I can't be bothered to go back, I have to train this girl and she's getting on my nerves. Why doesn't she speak?'

'Haha give her a list. You can put 'Say something' on it,' he laughs.

'Funny boy! I found out she's from Bulgaria, lives with her boyfriend and worked for an investment company before this. That's all I know.'

'So, you mean she doesn't talk an 'Elise' amount.'

'Shut up! You love it, otherwise you wouldn't be sitting here.'

'I mean, I have a very limited selection,' he laughs.

'You're such a prick,' I whine but I'm laughing too. I wonder if she would do a list. I doubt it. She'll probably think I'm mad anyway.

15.30

Right I've had enough, this is so painful. She's literally staring at the screen not saying anything. It's not nerves because she seems very confident. It's more like 'I am here to work' kind of silence.

After 10 minutes of nothing I can't help myself. 'So, I have been doing this thing called List Life – I give people a list or they give me one of five tasks to achieve within a 24-hour period, I can write you one if you like?'

Again, she stares straight at the screen and shrugs. Sod it, I am going to write one anyway, just for my own sanity.

16.45

I gave her a couple of jobs to work on over the past hour which has given me enough time to write her a list.

'So just before we leave, I have written you a list of things to complete in 24 hours, up to you if you want to do them, just a few fun things to do. It's not homework or anything,' I laugh and hand her a piece of paper that has been ripped from my note book. The list is:

Buy a scratch card

Draw or paint a portrait of someone you know

Text someone you haven't in a year

Do an online dance tutorial

Eat something posh or expensive

She didn't even look at it, she just folded it up, put it in her pocket and thanked me. But I don't care because finally it's the end of the day!

17.30

I'm so excited about tonight. I am going to see some old pals for Chinese food and catch up. I have known these girls since I was about five years old and we met at primary school. We were all so nerdy back then. But when I was nine, I moved away and we kept in touch, but not as often. We are all adults now (legally not mentally.) and we own cars, have our own places and trying to be adults as best we can. Every month or so we meet up and catch up on what we have been up to. Maybe I can get one of these girls to do a list. They are very sweet so it won't be as brutal as the pizza fiasco.

23.15

Well…they are definitely not nerdy now! Bianca is in Holland so we skyped her. She's found herself a great job and although she is having a few issues with her long-distance relationship she is loving life.

Ellen is single but it never stops her travelling. A born romantic she heads off on city breaks, meeting new people, drinking coffee in fancy pants coffee shops and staying in crazy unique hotels. She said she hitch-hiked to her last hotel. I'm not sure I am that brave.

Aimee and Viv are really happy together. Viv is thinking about moving down this way and they are looking to get a place together.

Most importantly they loved List Life! They were all buzzing about it and gave me a list to do tomorrow:

List 5 things you are grateful for

List 10 things you want to achieve by the time you are 40

Do something nice for your boss

Eat something you have always wanted to eat

Only drink water all day

Told you it would be tame. They are a really sweet bunch of girls and the list is deep and meaningful. I like it. I can do this one! But what I might struggle with is getting back from Ellen's. I am useless with directions and get lost everywhere I go. Wish me luck!

23.59

Finally, home but not easily! I was so excited that I'd come off at the right junction and could see the signs for home. I was doing my happy dance and turned the radio right up. Just as I found the right tune and was singing my heart out, I saw a police car up behind me flashing his lights. I pulled to the side of the road to let them past and they pulled over with me. They had pulled me over!

I panicked and assumed they had seen my happy dance and deemed it as dangerous driving (Obviously I wasn't doing the Mexican wave with both hands at the same time). I wound down the window when I saw a police officer approaching.

'Is this your car Miss?' He asked, quite sternly.

'Yes? Have I done something wrong?' I was shaking, I have never been approached by the police before.

'This car does not have a MOT, when was the last time you took it to the garage?'

'Erm, no idea actually, I suppose it is due a MOT.' I admit, under the pressure.

'If you could please step out of the vehicle and get into the police car, I just need to take some details from you.'

I was shaking when I locked up my car and headed towards the police car. He still had the lights flashing, bringing so much unnecessary attention to us. I was so nervous that without thinking I got in the front seat and sat on his ham and cheese sandwich.

'Oh my God, I'm so sorry' I panicked. I forgot you are meant to sit in the back in these situations but he seemed to think it was funny and told me to stay where I was while I gave him all my details. How embarrassing! Also, how annoying! A £60 fine. It was a really good night until then. Oh well, best sort this out tomorrow.

31st January

Kathy is on a diet so I can't buy her a cake or chocolate. I've stopped at the petrol station on the way to work and am about to buy her a scratch card BUT! What if she wins, I will be livid!

I hover in the sweet aisle and text the girls with my dilemma. Their response is:

That's the risk I face when being nice. So, I have to do it. God damn it! She best not win millions.

08.45

'Morning!' I sing, as a skip in, feeling like I am doing my good deed for the day.

Usual grunt response, as expected but I'm about to change that.

'I stopped at the shop and bought us both a scratch card, I didn't win anything on mine so fingers crossed you do.' I lie.

'Oh, that's nice Elise, what's this in aid of?' She takes the scratch card, and rummages around in her bag looking for a coin.

'No reason just a midweek treat, how's your son?'

'Yeah he was fine, just a disagreement about football that got out of hand, you know how kids are.' She says whilst scratching away at the card. Well no, not really, I don't really know anyone with kids apart from Molly and I can't imagine her son in a fight.

Kathy done her scratch card and won! But only £2, so now everyone's a winner. I also had to buy Tom and Monika something, otherwise it would have looked really weird. Tom loves a Twix so got them both one. Then I thought Bill would be the only one in early with them so got him a Snickers. Now it's cost me a small fortune. Never-the-less the gifts had been bought and everyone is happy, well apart from Monika she isn't in yet.

Normally I get in and make a cup of tea straightaway but as I am only allowed to drink water, I have had two glasses instead and have needed a wee every five minutes. The office is open plan and quite long which means everyone knows when you are going to the toilet. Looks like I have a problem.

09.18

Monika has still not arrived.

'Where's Monika?' I ask.

'She has called in sick today,' Tom blurts, even though the question was aimed at Kathy. Wow that's quick she was only for here one day. I wonder if she even looked at that list. Well at least I don't have to train her today, which is handy because I need to order some speakers, the sound team have been on at me about it for days.

10.30

Last night Viv seemed the most excited about List Life and has asked for a list today. Woohoo!

I don't actually have Viv's number as she is Aimee's girlfriend but I will send it to Aimee:

Make up a dance

Buy an unusual ornament

Learn how to say 'Will you marry me?' in Madarin.

Find out all about snails and then make a perfect house for one with all specifications

Text someone, telling them you love them (I know I have used that one before but it's a good one)

Send.

12.30

When I came back from grabbing another glass of water, Kathy is telling some of the guys from the warehouse about List Life. Aaron is mocking me and saying how ridiculous it is. They've been coming up with stupid suggestions and giggling like little school boys, it's so irritating.

Then Josh announces 'Ok, I will do you one!'

Shit!

A few things wrong with this:

1) They are team Kathy.

2) Although Brad is friends with them, when he hears about this, he is going to give me the 'It's not a stitch up' speech.

3) I am dreading what I will have to do.

I sit up straight, look them in the eye and say 'Game on!' I can do this.

I have now agreed to do Josh's list tomorrow and he will email it to me by end of play today (which is the most stupid saying. This is not play at all).

14.10

Brad isn't in. He's away in Switzerland on a job, so I have had to go on lunch on my own. I text Regina and they said they would have gone to lunch with me but they all work so far away and that would mean we only have 20 minutes together.

I'm now sitting in Morrison's café, on my own and eating macaroni cheese. I had all intentions of eating something really exotic as my 'something I have always wanted to eat' but I eat weird things all the time. Then I realised, I have never eaten macaroni cheese, so I thought now is the time. Turns out it's amazing! Why have I not had this before? Not a bad choice at all. Although, eating on my own is so horrible and I want to cry, I won't be doing this again. I can't bare seeing people eating on their own.

Once Jack and I were in a restaurant in Thailand and there was a guy sitting on his own at the table next to us. His beer came in a foam holder and he kept stroking it. At first, I thought it was really odd, then I saw a stick on the floor next to him and realised he was blind AND on his own. I cried so much that when the waitress came with our food, she was giving Jack the dirtiest looks so we had to eat and run. Admittedly, now I think back, we should have just spoken to him but he was probably quite happy there, eating his dinner, getting away from the wife for an hour or two and would have thought I was mad.

15.45

The scratch card worked. Kathy started being so nice to me and offered to get me a treat from the shop. She also asked what I was doing that evening and cracked jokes all day. Maybe the girls were right. I told you they were a nice bunch.

16.15

Bianca has text me to ask how the 'only drinking water' thing is going, which the answer is…badly! It turns out water all day is dangerous for my bladder. I'm like a sieve.

She also asked if I could do one for her! Woohoo this is spreading. I will do that later when I have finished this order.

16.30

I am placing an order for speakers and mics when an email from Josh appears.

Here is your list for tomorrow. Tenner says you don't do it all!

Walk to the end of Wincroft Avenue (the road we work on and I don't think anyone has ever been to the other side of the business park).

Apply to be on a game show

Eat dessert for breakfast

Invite Aaron for lunch

Buy a Goldfish and name him 'Josh the Great'

Bake Bread from scratch

Learn to juggle

Paint your nails an outrageous colour

Call a random friend then, when they answer, hang up and text them asking why they hung up

Get post-it notes and label everything on your desk

Jeez I forgot to tell him it had to be 5 things and it's really long but I will prove to him I can do it.

Let's do this!

17.45

Tonight, is Nan's night, which gives me time to pop back to Mum and Dad's and have a cup of tea with them.

I buzz on the doorbell and I can see my Dad walking towards the door, so I scramble about in my bag to pretend I am looking for my key. He opens the door and rolls his eyes.

'I'm not falling for that one. Where are your keys?' he laughs.

'I don't even live here anymore. Do I not get visitors rights?'

'No, you lazy thing, now come in, it's freezing,' he says and kisses me on the top of my head. 'How have you been?'

Mum makes me a cup of tea and I tell them all about the things I've been up to because it's been a busy few weeks. Making jewellery, eating mass pizza, investing money. They think it's great, plus they know I struggle in the winter with the cold and the dark. I told them how I set the boiler and made a cake and they are very impressed.

19.00

When I get to Nan's, the door is already open. I can hear her singing away.

'Nan?!' I call out because I don't want to make her jump.

'Come in! Dinners nearly ready!' she shouts back.

I let myself in and put my overnight bag down and head to the kitchen. As soon as she sees me, she grabs my arm and we start dancing around the kitchen. She's so fun!

When the song comes to an end, she grabs an oven glove ready to serve dinner. 'Elise, can you set the table and put Emmerdale on, please?'

We catch up on the madness in her place.

Apparently there is a lady downstairs and she has been seen with one of the men across the corridor gardening and having tea and his wife found out and there was a massive commotion in the laundry room last Thursday. It all kicked off.

Anyway, back to today's list. When were kids Ellen, Aimee, Bianca and I created a little club which involved us going around each other's house on a Tuesday to make crafty things (Told you we were nerdy. We were only 7 though). Anyway, this club was called SEAT club made up of the first letter of our surnames. So, Bianca list is:

Design a logo for a new SEAT club

Give a red envelope to someone with a nice message in it

Do the workout to Bianca (the alphabet workout used earlier)

Buy something for Jai (her boyfriend) *but it has to be green*

Eat 20 sweets of any sort.

20.05

In between watching the soaps and chatting to Nan, I have written my list of the things I am grateful for today:

1 – Having a boyfriend who is tolerant, loyal and actually likes me

2 – That I am able to come to my Nan's every week

3 – That my pals wanted to go on lunch with me today

4 – For the food I ate (porridge, macaroni and cheese, lamb chops, potatoes and broccoli)

5 – That there are people joining me on List Life

And the things I will do before I am 40

1 - Be fluent in two different languages (first I will master Spanish then maybe Japanese)

2 – Travel to every continent (I said to Jack we cannot get married until this one is complete)

3 – Have children

4 – Own a business (maybe that can be my beer stall, if I ever manage to do it)

5 – Own a house

6 – Have a job I love (working on it)

7 – Have a good body (failing to work on it)

8 – Have all jabs so I am travel-ready for everywhere

9 – Get married (only if number two is complete)

10 – Learn to dance

10.30

'Not one number!' Nan growls all frustrated.

She does the lottery every week, and makes me watch the News while we wait for it to come on. I love it when she wins, even if it's a little bit because we can get all excited. It's the little things that make you happy. Although I do hope she wins big one day.

We always go to bed early when I stay round and it always makes me feel so refreshed in the morning. Tomorrow I will get up ready for Josh's list.

Night guys x

Chapter 8 – Game on!

1st Feb

07.00

Few more things that are amazing about staying at Nan's:

1 – I get to sleep in an extra 45 mins because she lives closer to the office.

2 – She makes me egg on toast every week (but this week I have to have dessert but won't make her knock me up a cheesecake)

3 – She gets up and plays old school songs on the new Bluetooth speakers she got from my uncle at Christmas.

4 - When I leave, she always stands at the door waving and says 'Bye sweetie, have a great day.'

And I believe I will.

08.28

I have been at work for half an hour and my desk looks such a mess. I have labelled everything and Kathy is going to flip her lid when she sees it!

On my way in I popped into the bakery and picked up a chocolate éclair for breakfast and it was actually amazing! I might do that every day. Probably get heartburn in 10 minutes but it was well worth it.

08.48

I am getting through these ones before Kathy arrives and tells me I can't use the computer for non-work-related stuff, like applying for 'Dream Big'. Never heard of it, never watched it but I could be going on the show if I am successful. I hope I don't get chosen but I would have to do it because it relates to the list, I would die of embarrassment being on TV.

09.06

Hmmm, Monika still isn't in. Apparently, she called in sick again today. Well that's not a good start is it? Imagine if I took a few days off, Kathy would be losing her mind. Oh well! Can't judge. She might be really ill or I scared her off this with the list. It *was* a bit too much but I couldn't think what else to talk to her about.

I will pop to the toilet to make a call to Will because I know he is the only one that will pick up.

'Hi Bitch, what do you want?' Well, I think I might hang up anyway seeing as he is so rude.

Text him straight after: *Why did you hang up?!*

Shut up! You hung up on me! Anyway, what you up to next week. Do you want to meet up? I'm down that way, to cover for another store.

Yesss lets do this. What do you fancy doing?

I'm staying at my Dad's so somewhere round there.

Perfecto!

HA! Stitch up failed Josh. I am now making plans unintentionally.

13.30

Aaron has agreed to go to lunch with me and Josh has decided he wants to tag along, which I think we are both equally pleased about. It would have been really odd otherwise and I have a plan! I will drag them both to the end of Wincroft avenue as part of our lunch and see if there is a café or something up there. Kills two birds with one stone! Now we are waiting for Josh to send an email before we can leave.

13.42

We start walking up the road and it isn't that awkward to be fair. They're just chatting about the lists and having a laugh about it. I can see the end of the road and there is just a roundabout which allows cars turn around…what a waste of time!

'Shall we just go to Costco instead?' Josh suggests.

We both agree and I'm quite excited about it because it's just around the corner from the office and everyone raves that you can get a massive jacket potato for £1.50 with 2 fillings but I have never been. They both offer to drive which is great because my car is so disgusting. MOT all up to date now though thankfully.

13.50

As soon as we order our food and sit down it takes all of two seconds before Aaron crow-bars in a conversation about Brad.

'Yeah, I didn't think anyone would have noticed to be honest but we have been at it for months,' I casually say and carry on eating.

Josh stops mid-bite and looks at Aaron. Aaron is staring at me 'Are you serious?'

'Yeah, for sure. I mean wasn't it obvious?!'

'Well yeah but…' Then he notices Josh laughing (who I have already winked at) and pulls that 'very funny' face to which I roll my eyes and laugh. Why is everyone so obsessed.

Apart from that 10 second interrogation all these guys talk about is work. It's so boring! They are only young, don't they have football to talk about or some hot girl in the office? Oh well Brad is back tomorrow so I can go on lunch with him. He text me earlier to say that Jeremy (this right prick of a manager) had slipped on the ice 4 times aaahaha!!!

15.40

I have been trying to persuade Jack into getting a fish for the past hour. He seems pretty up for it but says he wants to do it at the weekend when we can both go out and choose one.

Crap! It needs to be within 24 hours otherwise it defeats the 24-hour list.

'How about I get one fish and all the stuff today and then at the weekend we can go out and get another fish and buy really cool stuff for it?'

'OK, I'm not going to win, am I? Do what you've got to do, List Queen.'

I think that's reasonable. I feel bad because he puts up with so much but if I fail at this it will make the list thing look like a silly game and the guys will think I am a joke; well they already do, but more so.

18.15

What a drama! I arrive at the pet shop, which, by the way is the complete opposite direction to home so it means I am going to be back so late to do the rest of my challenges.

I walk in and look around at all the different fish. I choose my favourite one and head to the checkout point. Josh the Great has a really dramatic tail and looks, well, 'Great'.

When I get to the counter, I ask the woman if I can buy one of the fish in tank 4. I try to sound like I know what I'm doing.

'Do you have a tank?' She looks at me as if she has sussed that I have never bought a fish before or any living creature for that matter.

'No, can I have one of those too please and some fish food?'

Well apparently, turns out you have to have a tank and filter for three days before buying a fish. Also, they need a tank, a filter, food, cleaning products...fussy little things. So 'Josh the Great' will have to be bought at the weekend after all. I purchased the tank and other accessories anyway, in preparation for his arrival. Technically not a fail.

I'm just going to pop next door to the pound shop to get my bright nail varnish.

19.30

So, I'm home and the tank is all set up but the noise is ridiculous and the filter keeps popping out of the top. I have never been the pet type but I will have to be now. I'm paranoid that this will affect my holidays and I will feel like one of those people who has to get someone to come in to feed the fish. Maybe Alfie and Samantha can do it. They don't live far. At least it won't need to be walked twice a day.

On a lighter note I have bright yellow nails. They look disgusting but rules are rules.

20.00

'Oh shit!' I curse. Jack has just walked in and I am covered in flour, brushing it off my face and pasting it through my hair.

'What are you doing now Mary Berry?' he laughs. 'Is this another list?'

'Yes, I have to make bread.' I shove the dough in the oven, I have never attempted bread before so I have no idea how this will come out. I thought you might need a machine or something but turns out it's not that hard to do, well, if it works.

'Now do you know where my phone is? I need to find a tutorial on how to juggle!' I explain whilst rummaging through my bag.

'I know how to juggle,' he says as he places his rucksack in the bedroom and takes his coat off 'I have to teach the kids how to juggle in school.'

'Do you? I didn't know you could juggle.'

'Yeah, course.' he picks up three lemons. 'You just have to throw one lemon up and swap the other one into the right hand and then keep repeating that.'

He does it so well! Lemons flowing round in a perfect circle. I never knew he could do that. How impressive! He laughs and winks at me…. Oh, jeez he looks so cool!

When he passes me the lemons, I chuck one straight over my shoulder. God dammit! Why can I never do anything?

'Right, do it slowly,' he instructs.

After a few embarrassing attempts, I'm off juggling like a pro! I thought this was going to be the hardest one but it turns out I have a sexy sports coach to teach me. Is juggling a sport?

BEEEP! The oven alarms and I jump and throw the lemons in the air. My bread is ready!

I nervously take it out the oven and… Oh My God! It's amazing! It looks just like bread. I go running in the living room with the loaf 'Look! Look! I've done it!'

'Wow that looks amazing, Oh! I can make a stew tomorrow and we can use it to scoop it up with. I have a job in central so can come home earlier.'

'Yess, Oh, this is so cool! I can't wait until tomorrow to show everyone at work. List Life is the best thing ever!' and I skip back into the kitchen.

23.45

Before I go to bed, I will text Brad because I'm so excited:

Josh and Aaron may laugh and feel like they have stitched me up but today I have eaten a really nice cake for breakfast, applied for a TV show, ruined their lunch, painted my nails, baked my first ever loaf of bread, learnt to juggle, sent Will a text and we are now meeting up.

What! Josh and Aaron?

Oh shit! I forgot to tell him they had given me a list.
Well Kathy was telling them about it yesterday and Josh emailed me one. It was really long, had nine things on it but I did all the things I just told you about, so it worked out well.

Nine things? Isn't it meant to be five?

Well kind of, but that was my rule.

Why are they even getting involved? And why does everyone put something that stops us going to lunch?

Well, both times you have been away anyway, so it didn't matter. Anyway, be happy for me. I succeeded and I proved them wrong!

Go you! he replies, but I can sense the sarcasm.

Right! I'm going to bed I'm knackered after all that.
Buenas Noches!

Chapter 9 – Back in the game!

2nd Feb

06.39

Brad is back today and I have actually felt sorry for him. He is a Project Manager and some of the technicians that were sent out to Switzerland fell ill so he had to step in and he's been working really long nights. Apparently, it's been freezing and the onsite food has been a choice of either standard lasagne and chips or curry and cold rice, so I'm giving him a list for the day to make him feel better and to get him feeling good again.

Clean all the windows in your flat (I know it sound like a chore but the sun will shine in and make him feel fresh)

Eat dinner with 3 superfoods (This will make him feel fit and healthy again)

Find an experience or anything from Groupon and arrange to do it with a mate (Communication with people he likes, not just work colleagues)

Find your favourite photo of yourself and send it to me by tomorrow evening (This a weird one. 1) It will give him something to do so he doesn't end of watching TV in the evening and 2) The memories will make him happy, and maybe sad due to the ex-wife thing. He might even cry but then he will sleep better.

Text me every 4 hours with an interesting fact about your last 4 hours. (Just for the hell of it)

Ask Bill to teach you something (Just for a wind up really)

06.50

'*Fine, but YOU need to do this one'*

Only eat in multiples of three

On the hour, every hour from 9-5, either arrange to meet a pal or book a lesson in something (can mix and match)

Either join a gym or draw up a workout routine for the next week

Write your nan a letter

Tell Regina you are now a practicing Buddhist.

Draw Jack a picture and give it to him before he goes to bed

See this is why I like Brad's lists. None of them take the piss and they're always slightly productive.

08.02

I bounce into the office so smug and proud of myself with my loaf of bread and place it in front of Josh. Booom!

'Wow, to be fair, I didn't think you would do it. Did you get the fish?'

'Well, I couldn't buy one last night because you need the tank for three days but I have it all set up now and will get one on Saturday.'

'Come on then, let me try the bread' He nods towards the kitchen.

Normally I would be fuming that he has ordered me around but I want him to try it more than he does so I rush off to the kitchen.

Once word gets around, everyone wants a slice of the bread. Well, this is how you make friends in here is it? Who would have known it? Wow, I am actually an amazing baker! Tom loves it and has two pieces and even toasts them.

I lather mine with butter and manage to eat it in six bites which is a multiple of three, making sure I do this list properly.

09.00

Right first plan of the day.

Hi Molly! How's it going? Are you free anytime next week? I could pop over after work? Or maybe we can go to the pub for dinner?

Hopefully she'll say yes. I haven't seen her and her son in ages, would be good to catch up.

10.30

Text Regina…

Does anyone want to do breakfast Saturday?

Zee: *Yessss lets do this!*

Rosie: *Can we go to that new place in town? It opened last Friday.*

Me: *Yes, but, by the way I'm a now a Buddhist, just in case that affects breakfast plans.*

Dawn: *Why would that affect breakfast and is that what you were going to show us yesterday?*

Me: *Oh no I was meant to buy a fish but couldn't because I needed a tank for three days.*

Rosie: A fish! What is wrong with you! If you're going to get a pet, get a dog.

Me: No, I am terrified of dogs and have a one-bed flat!

Zee: *You know Buddhists are veggies though Hun?*

Me: *Fuck!*

Dawn: *She can't give up the sausage!*

Booom! The girls are on it! Breakfast sorted. I will tell them I'm not an actual Buddhist before then.

10.20

I text Brad: *Jeez you are so late today, where are you? I got you some bread. You are going to miss out.*

So, I had to get the DLR to Excel which was built in 1987 and I believe is still the only fully automated railway in the UK. I wasn't there long but I did get to talk to Professor Brian Cox! It's not been the most fun week so far but, interestingly, I managed to rearrange my day so I could try and change that... how is that part of my four hours you ask...well?

Eh? What is he talking about? Then, when I look up, he is standing there looking at me all pleased with himself.

'Clever'... I roll my eyes.

What's clever? Kathy grunts at me.

Oh shit, didn't mean to say that out loud. 'Oh, nothing I just found a button on the system that I didn't know about.' She just shakes her head and makes another flirty phone call to one of the delivery men. Honestly, it's embarrassing.

By the way Monika still hasn't come back to work, she must be seriously ill or given up with this place. I don't blame her.

11.18

It's past 11.00am and I need to think of another plan or course. Hmmm… Oh wait! I could learn how to sail then I could meet new yachting pals.

I found one that is too expensive but they have a free trial so I signed up! I get a 6 month pass so maybe I should do that one in the summer when it's a bit warmer.

My previous yachting experience hasn't been great. Once I decided to help out at my brother's scouts' group when we were kids and they did a family sailing day. I got in a boat with my brother and half way across the lake our boat capsized. It wasn't dangerous, we could stand up, but the water was freezing and there was so much goose poo all over the bottom of the lake it was horrible. I refuse to give up on the idea but I think summer would be the best time for sailing.

12.37

I'm so bored! It's a quiet time of the year so most of the work is updating systems and planning for the year ahead!

Brad texts: *In a meeting and I'm bored. Tell me something interesting.*

Women have to hold onto the cubicle walls and guide themselves down to the toilet when drunk.

Sexiest mental image ever, he replies.

It's never a sexy scene Brad.

I don't understand women's toilets. Why does it take so long for you girls to go for a wee?

Brad! The girl's toilets are the social hub of any night out! We all become friends, lending each other makeup, giving our new found friends drunken advice about the guy they've just met, then someone shouts that they have run out of loo roll and we create a relay system where a donated roll is flying over and under the cubicle walls.

But! We must not forget the leader of this fiesta! The... Toilet Attendant/Party Starter and most importantly, provider of all essentials – deodorant, gum, makeup and Chubba-Chubba lolly pops.

Lolly pops?

Yeah, I never get that one either. Anyway, hurry I want to go to lunch!

13.45

Crap! With all that talk of girl's toilets, I forgot to book something. Hmm what can I do? I scan the internet for fun activities and the one that keeps popping up is salsa classes. I used to work in a pub and they held salsa classes every Wednesday. It did look quite fun. I will ask my pals if they want to come with me.

Salsa? Natalie replies instantly.

Isn't that for old people? Tanya joins in.

No! It looks cool and a bit up close and personal with hot Spanish men.

I'm in! Haha knew that would change her mind.

Do I have to do this or is it a girl's thing? Please say it's just a girl's thing. Graham begs.

Nope! We need a partner so you are coming along too. There's one near you guys on a Thursday night in town. Shall we give it a go next week? It's only £6.

Oh, sod it! Why not! But let's go for a drink first to 'relax'. Graham suggests.

Ok deal, see you guys Thursday! How exciting!

14.02

We take a trip into town because I need my eyebrows done. This poor boy gets dragged around everywhere. He is updating me on goss from the Switzerland trip. Apparently, it was so cold that he felt ill and Jeremy fell over another eight times aahahaha, this has made my day. He's not the nicest man so I don't feel bad about laughing.

I also booked a course on investing so I will finally be rich!

14.39

Brad sent me his four-hour update: *When I got into work, I had to have a meeting as there were four near fatal accidents on site in Switzerland and I'm the only one who flagged them! Then, I was browsing for courses and found a sailing course which I want to do this summer and you were banging on about it at lunch! Talking of lunch, I discovered we can get to town and back within the boring allocated lunch hour so everything is all good.*

15.04

Kathy is in another meeting about nothing and Tom is in an unusually chatty mood. We have been trying to come up with another course or plan and have decided on knitting. Tom is actually very good at knitting; he has knitted me a scarf and jumper for Christmas. I keep telling him he should sell the things he knits but he said he's not interested and just wants to do it as a hobby. Once he knitted loads of tiny new born baby hats for pre-mature babies. How nice is that? He lives with his sister who is a lot older and I think she teaches him. They are amazing knitters!

16.30

Last plan of the day is going to be with my Mum.

Mum are you free this weekend to go to Bhaktivedanta Manor?

Ooo yes! I have always wanted to go there! Shall we say 12?

I am having breakfast with the girls so I will pick you at 1! I suggest.

Perfect!

Great so that's a plan or a course each hour.

17.00

Text Brad: *To be fair I'm back in the game today.*

Were you out of the game? he asks.

Yeah yesterday I felt like the List Life had pissed Jack off about the fish and thought it would piss you off me going to lunch with Josh and Aaron when you knew they were trying to stitch me up, so I was going to give the whole game up, but it turned out ok and I have done the list!

No don't listen to anyone. You are smashing it!

Ok good, I will carry on.

17.45

No traffic! Back to a cosy, warm flat and buzzing off life.

In the last four hours Brad got a message from his crew saying that the job they did in Switzerland was great and that he was a good leader. Then he got an email from the festival he is playing at, asking how many he wanted on his guest list and their dietary requirements. Who does he think he is? (He is a keyboard player in a heavy metal band and they are doing pretty well. They are playing at a big festival soon I think).

19.00

Jack is watching football and I am making my jewels, doing what we do best! Both very happy and very content.

I love making jewellery, it's very therapeutic, even if no one buys it.

21.41

Well this night has taken a weird turn. It started off with me making jewellery, loving life. Then I started writing my Nan a letter and ended up a blubbering mess. I'm cold as ice in some situations and then, when I think too much, I end up a right melt. It wasn't even sad, I just realised how much I love her and how cool she is. Very lucky to have her. In fact, I am lucky to have both my Nan's and one Grandad and I see them on a regular basis.

My Nan and Grandad on my Dad's side are just as amazing! They have a campervan and go all over the country. They love Chinese food and a good bottle of red. Grandad is a member of the lake's fishing crew, the darts team and goes out on his bike whenever he can. Nan goes shopping with her best pal Rose and they are part of a ten-pin bowling club. She's got her own bowling ball and a pretty sleek pair of bowling shoes.

I call my Mum's Mum 'Little Nan' and my Dad's Mum 'Big Nan' No idea why! Just a weird way to distinguish them as a kid.

22.00

Brad has sent me a number of hilarious photos of himself because he is trying to find his best photo of himself but is also got emotional because he has found photos of his ex-wife, which I knew would happen. It's a good to get emotional now and again. He also saw loads of photos of him playing in various bands, holidaying with friends and wearing very questionable outfit choices.

I've found 'The One'. It's a photo of him in the desert in Dubai, standing next to an off road four x four. It's a pretty cool photo to actually. He has wild, curly hair anyway but where the wind has caught it, it looks crazy and makes it quite a powerful photo. Good choice.

I have no up-to-date photos of myself. He moans.

We'll get one this week, we can take one at lunch!

Sure, sounds good. Windows done! Just desperately browsing Groupon. Have you drawn your picture yet?

Yep, I drew our uni logo, a plane and our flat to represent our relationship, uni, travel and moving in together.

Now that's a melt!

Oi! So, what were your last four hours like?

I cooked a wicked meal with three superfoods – fish cooked with olive oil and made a sauce using turmeric. Cleaned my windows. Luckily most of my windows are small apart from the balcony doors so it was ok. I then booked an 18-hole golf thing even though

I am not a golfer but be fun to do something different. I think Dave may bail, but if he does, my Dad would appreciate it, so I think I'm covered.

I explain that I have finished half a bottle of wine and drank it in three glasses because rules are rules. Then I get a text about five minutes later.

I just realised that I have been stressed all week but now I feel so relaxed and that's why you made me eat superfoods and clean so that I felt better.

For sure, did it work?

Yeah, I feel great! Elise, can you do me a favour?

Sure!

Can you write me a list for Monday, I'm loving it!

One step ahead of ya boy…here goes:

Practice being a Buddhist for the day

You are also a veggie

Throw a party for Mr Chow because it's his birthday (he told me this the other day I didn't just make it up, I'm not sure how he knows a hamster's birthday).

Do one thing you thought was cool when you were looking at your photos.

Wow ok done! Night Bitch.

Wait! Transfer me £5.00 and trust me, I add.

Hmmm, ok send me your bank details and I will do it in the morning.

Wow that is trust!

You know what? I feel just as relaxed. Sometimes I need a list from Brad because I know he isn't going to try and trip me up or make me do anything horrible. Don't get me wrong, the other lists are fun and challenging but he was the inspiration for the original list and knows what it's meant to be like.

3rd Feb

09.00

It's Saturday and I am up early and, on my way to meet Regina for breakfast. We are meeting in town at the new place Rosie suggested. I park up and head over to see Zee waiting outside, having a cigarette. She spots me and stumps it out waving her arms around, ready to give me a hug. I don't do greeting hugs and she knows this but decides to ignore it.

'Heyyy! I haven't seen you in ages, how've you been?' Zee always sounds so excited and happy.

'Hey! I'm good but I'm starving. Are the others here yet?' I ask, because I really want to get inside, its freezing.

'Dawn just text to say that she's parking up so let's go in and get a table.' I think my face must have said it all.

10.15

When the others arrive, we order straight way, knowing full well that we have all already looked at the menu online.

'Could I have the pancakes with bacon please?' I order.

Rosie has ordered some fancy avocado dish and the others go for a full English.

'Could we also have four mimosas too, please?' Dawn asks.

'Woah, sorry. What are we celebrating? I thought this was just breakfast!'

'Well…' She has a massive grin on her face and then out of nowhere she is displaying her hand in the middle of the table. The diamond is huge!

We all gasp in unison.

'Oh my god! Congratulations!' Zee is obviously the first to lean over and give her a hug.

'Wow, how did he did do it?' I ask, because, although weddings and engagements has never been my thing, it has definitely been Dawn's dream and I bet she can't wait to tell us.

'Well we went down to my parents holiday apartment in Devon last weekend just for a few days. Then for dinner he had hired out a booth in this really fancy restaurant, which I thought was odd, but wasn't complaining. Once we had eaten and had a few drinks we walked along the beach front and out of nowhere he got down on one knee and proposed. Obviously, I said yes straight away. Then when we got back to the apartment, he had arranged for my whole family to be there and we had a little party to celebrate.'

'Aww' we cry.

'But that's not all! My Mum then handed me her phone and showed me the video of the 'moment'. They had been sitting on a bench a little way down the beach and he had arranged for them to film it so I could look back on it.'

'AWW!' We cry again but a little louder.

'Let me see it again!' Rosie grabs her hand and is analysing the ring. It is a nice ring – silver with a huge rock.

We spend the rest of the morning discussing venues, bridesmaids' dresses and my favourite topic – potential honeymoon destinations. At 12.30 I say that I have to leave because I am meeting Mum but they seem to be eager to head off too. Dawn has an appointment to look at wedding dresses with her sister, Rosie is going to see if she can sort things out with Kevin and Zee says she has a date tonight so is off to get her nails done.

13.05

When I pull up to Mum's, I give her a call. I would get out but it's raining and I don't want to get cold and wet.

She climbs into the car and shakes of her umbrella before closing the door.

'I am so excited about going here! I have driven past it so many times it looks amazing!' She is buzzing.

'I know same!' I say excitedly, as we head off.

On the way there, which is only a 20-minute drive, she tells me that my brother Harvey brought his new girlfriend over to dinner last night and it turns out Ava knew her from an audition she went to once. She sounds like a nice girl and works as a makeup artist in one of the local theatres so has given Ava and Mum tickets for a musical next week. Thank god she didn't get me one.

When we arrive, the carpark is so confusing so I get lost but there is a very nice man who asks if we are attending the religious event or just visiting? We explain that we have never been before and we have just come to look around.

Bhaktivedanta Manor is a Hare Krishna temple and it looks amazing. Beautiful grounds and a huge house welcome to anyone.

We are asked to take off our shoes and head to the reception.

'Hello and welcome,' the lady at reception says in an almost whisper.

'Hello, we are just visiting and wondered if we could have a look around?' Mum asks.

'Of course, if you wait here for a few minutes, I will find someone to take you around.' The lady perks up. She looks just as excited as us.

After a few minutes of us scanning the gift shop, a tall man dressed in a white linen shirt, brown linen trousers and bare feet approaches us.

'Hello ladies, are you here for a tour?' he asks.

'Yes please, would that be ok? I have always wanted to come here. It's beautiful' Mum explains, almost apologetically.

'I would love to show you around. We have many visitors every day' and he leads us off around the manor.

It's incredible, high ceilings and grand décor. There are so many rooms and everyone we pass greets us with a smile. The tour guide explains the history of the Hare Krishna movement and how the manor is used nowdays.

At the end of the tour he takes us to a massive prayer room and says we can join in with everyone if we would like to stay and then mentions that there is food served in the room next door afterwards. I mean you don't have to ask me twice when it comes to trying new food.

The experience in the prayer room is fascinating but also hilarious because Mum and I have no idea what we were doing and keep looking at each other for reassurance that we were doing it right. When the service was over, we follow everyone into another room where food is being served. There is a short queue and when we get to the food stations, we hold out our plates which is being filled with loads of crazy, amazing dishes. I have no idea what everything is but that's what I love about it.

There are no seats and everyone is sitting on the floor so we find a spot and make ourselves comfortable.

'Wow this food is amazing!' I gush.

'I know. What is this sauce? It's delicious!' Mum is dipping her bread in a thick greenish pulp.

'It's so cool here, we should walk round the gardens when we have finished if you have time and it's not raining still?'

'Yeah, of course! Thank you for asking me here. Was it on your list?' she laughs.

'No but it did stem from a list – I had to make a plan on the hour every hour and this was one of them. I'm glad I chose it now.'

'It's beautiful.'

We finish our food and find the tour guide to thank him. He gives us some flyers about up and coming events. Then we head out to the gardens which are equally incredible.

I go back to Mum's for a cup of tea while we excitedly tell Dad all about our day in true woman fashion – talking over each other and getting faster and faster.

It's been such a good day but I need to head home now. Jack will be wondering where I am.

5th Feb

06.30

Monday again and my alarm has been going off every 10 mins for the last hour, I just can't bring myself to get up. I'm so tired and the thought of going to see those loons is not helping. Sort yourself out Elise. I whip back the duvet…and I'm up! Jack always looks so happy when he's sleeping… he's such a chilled-out guy. Aww! Think he's struggling living with me at the moment… Oh well, like I always tell him - You knew what is was when you signed up.

08.35

Traffic today was painful. The M25 is a nightmare at this time of the morning.

When Brad gets in, he's rolling his eyes at me. Then a text pings on my phone

Meditation is so hard.

Hahaha so that's why he's so late. Try explaining that to Steve – Who has been moaning about the traffic for 10 minutes now. We were all stuck in it mate! Pipe down.

Why are you meditating? I text back.

Because I'm a Buddist today. He looks up at me over the desk and fling his arms up as if it's obvious.

Oh yeah! The list! I forgot about that one, I flick through my notes on my phone to remind myself what I put on the list.
So, what do Buddhists have to do then?

It's complicated but basically, I can't kill, steal or break promises.

Well this is going to be a difficult day for him!
Also, I can only eat meat if it's offered to me, which I actually can't because I'M A VEGGIE today.

Kathy is in a grumpy, 'not talking' mood so I will email you today rather than text.

Told you it wouldn't last.

Is Mr Chow excited about tonight?

Well he's around my parents, because they fed him while I was away, so will have to do it there.

Hilarious.

11.03
Monika is finally back in today, but still isn't talking. I didn't ask

why she was off, just asked if she felt better. Tom has been talking to her all morning about some paranormal activity he experienced last night. I swerve right out the way of that convo.

Kathy seems so aggy about work. She can't seem to figure out why the figures are adding up wrong on an invoice and is being so snappy with everyone.

Brad has obviously noticed too: *Mate, Kathy is a (and sends a picture of a chicken)*

A chicken? What is he on about?

*No, a C**K but I'm not allowed to say it because I'm a Buddhist and I'm not allowed to say or look at anything sexual.*

Wow, that's messed up your evening then, haha

Ha...Funny girl.

Oi, when are we going to lunch? I'm starving!

Calm down! It's only 11am. Let's go at the normal time 1.30, come and get a Jaffa cake. I have loads.

As I get up, she snaps again. 'Where are you going?'

'Going to the toilet' I lie. 'Do you need me for anything?'

'Just hurry back, we are busy!'

Oh bejeez, what is wrong with her today. Even Monika laughs a bit when I roll my eyes because it's so embarrassing.

13.30

This woman is being such a Bitch today! She knows I go to lunch with Brad at 1.30 and she's asking him a million questions about a gig we are doing in 2 months' time. I mean, it can wait an hour. She just thinks she can mess up our lunch. Well she can't. I'll wait for him.

13.55

Is she joking! I'm so hungry? I have been waiting, clicking in and out of screens trying to make myself look busy for 25 minutes while she is asking him how many cables would be best for this new screen that has come on the market? We don't need to know this; we don't even have it ordered yet!

14.15

She won! I'm too hungry for this game. I'm going to get some sushi and then go clothes shopping for China...how exciting! Do you think I should buy Chinese style clothes? Or is that weird? Maybe I can just buy some out there! I love anything cultural, whether it be their food, clothes, music, anything I love it! If someone says something's traditional, I will buy it. Tourist traps dream.

15.15

So, I didn't get any clothes BUT I did get 3 pairs of earrings and a necklace. I know I shouldn't buy any more jewellery, especially as I am now making it but it made me happy.

Now back to the hell hole…

16.12

I'm shaking with anger. I had to come in the toilets just to get away from her! My heart is pounding and my arms are pulsing with adrenaline. How can she single me out like that in front of everyone! Brad was laughing too and even Tom was laughing and that's unheard of! Just because she wasn't involved.

The intercom had rung and Tom answered it and had an air bubble so his voice came out really squeaky. We all laughed because it was hilarious but she scowled at me and growled:

'Elise your sniggering is very off-putting, please concentrate!'

I was shocked! Everyone was laughing and then they were all looking at me waiting for my reply. The whole office was now dead silent and looking for my reaction:

'Oh jeez Kathy! We were only having a laugh.' I snapped and she snapped back 'Yes but some of us have work to do and your laugh is getting on my nerves.'

So now I'm in the ladies debating if I can leave now and just find another job after China. I have saved up £200 and I will get paid until the end of the month anyway so it is possible. I use the calculator on my phone taking away my rent and bills, petrol and clothes for China. Oh, and those shoes I saw the other day, minus the tickets I bought for the Red Hot Chili Peppers gig at the end of the year. Hmm, I probably shouldn't walk out now but maybe I should start looking for another job as I've been here eight months and I hate it already. I have the stroppiest boss in the entire world, the men are so boring and it's not like Monika is going to my bestie. I've had enough!

When I get back to my desk Brad is looking at me all sympathetic and Tom asks if I want to go to the kitchen for a cup of tea? YES, of course I do because I don't want to see that crazy woman any more than I need to.

Bless Tom he is an absolute nutter, but he's heart is in the right place. He said he will speak to his spiritual guide, Moon-shadow, who is a goat apparently and he will know what to do. He said Kathy is being very hard on me and I don't deserve it. He said he will find out what I should do. Haha…good old Moon-shadow.

He can ask Moon-shadow for this week's lottery numbers while he's at it because I need some luck!

17.30

Yess, home time finally! I need to pop to the shops on the way home so I hope there's no traffic.

18.16

I'm in this cool outlet store I pass everyday but have never been in. My plan is that with the £5.00 Brad sent me I'm going to buy a frame and frame the photo he sent me. Then he has his favourite photo of himself framed. See I can be cute!

There are two frames: one plain black and one with a cool orange pattern but I don't know how his flat is decorated and boys always like boring colours. Black it is! Now that's sorted I'm going to go home.

19.14

Text from Brad: *List your 3 oldest pals and a fact about each of them.*

Ooo that's an interesting one. Hmmm... ok Bianca. She used to have a cuckoo clock and when I stayed round there when I was about seven, I stayed up all night all night because I loved it when the clock struck the hour.

Then there's Ellen - I know her because my Dad and her Dad are besties and been since they were seven and grew up together. Her fact is that when we were kids, she won a drawing competition. The prize was a meal with a friend and she chose me (and her parents) and I have always thought it was somewhere posh until a year ago her mum told me it was only a supermarket cafe.

And last, but not least, Aimee. She used to have a dog called Dipsy and I was terrified of him even though he was a tiny little Shih-Tzu.

How about me? What if someone said tell me a fact about Brad, what would you say?

Ermm, I would say he can fly a plane or he is in a band. How about me?

Funny enough I described you the other day to Dave and I said you eat something new from the world food aisle each week.

Wish I could eat from a different country each week. I feel like I need to go travelling again or something. I feel bored with going to work, then home, then work, then home again. Real life is boring but I know travel isn't real life.

Real life is what you make it so don't be duped into doing things because they're 'normal' or 'right'. Live how you need to live. It's never too late to do anything. Everyone is different and that's a good thing. You say you want a business, so fight for it. Maybe find a way of doing it on Saturdays while Jack is at work. Also, you've just moved into your own place so you need to give it time for that to develop.

I know I'm hard to live with because I don't want to sit in. I want to do things all the time and I know it comes across as selfish.

I've never met Jack but he knows who you are and what you are about because you've been together eight years! You're strong-willed, stubborn and independent but you're not selfish...enough deep talk. I told my mum we have to throw a party for the hamster as it's his birthday and she has turned the house upside down looking for decorations! It looks pretty good we have a party table cloth and bunting haha.

WHAT A LEDGE! Mrs Evans is on board.

We have apple pie instead of cake though.

That's fine. How's it feel being a Buddhist?

It's quite cool actually, I've learnt a lot about it. Mum made a veg curry but I need to go home and meditate now. I also want to rock out on my keyboard! What are you doing tonight?

I'm making more jewellery. It's quite therapeutic. Also, I have a charity stall this weekend that I am doing with Jack's Mum.

Well I'm just about to head off home. Enjoy your jewellery making.

Laters.

I have made 40 pairs of earrings and 30 necklaces. My eyes hurt but I have finally finished.

I feel like I need to rest my eyes but I have the urge to Facebook stalk this Monika girl. There's something about her that's odd, not in a creepy way, but in a mysterious way. Ah! I found her! There's a lot of selfies! She is stunning. I'd take more selfies if I looked like her. Just like in person, her profile gives nothing away, but it does say that she moved to England in 2014 so she's only been living in the England a few years. Oh, this is boring now. I will go and read Yes Man! I know, it's taking me ages, I'm a slow reader.

23.10

Just as I'm sitting in bed Brad text again*: So, I'm home now and my thing in the past was dressing up in outrageous costumes and playing music. What do you think?*

Oh, Good God! He's in a mesh black vest and skin tight animal print trousers!

*1) You look ridiculous and 2) I used to know a guy that used to dress like that...you scare m*e!

Me? How?

You're in tiger print leggings Brad...

Listen, when I was about twenty-one, I used to play gigs like this and 300 people were singing my songs and a hot barmaid gave me 50p pints all night so I feel this is a winning outfit. I'm going to play one song now and then take them off. They are a little tighter than I remember.

Did you watch First Dates tonight? There was a guy on there that was wearing a similar outfit.

I was watching that but it got a bit racy so I had to turn it off. I'm still a Buddhist for the next 15 minutes.

Hahaha, good, don't break the rules.

Mum texted asking what you thought of the party we had thrown for Mr Chow?

Amazing you went all out ...LIST LIFE!

We made it, we live it, we rule it!

Chapter 10 – The little things

10th February

The local church is hosting a fete to raise money for local church volunteers to go to Sri Lanka and take part in community activities such as working with locals and helping in schools etc. I didn't realise they did things like that. How cool!

I meet Jack's Mum at the church hall and we set up our table full of my jewellery and bits she has collected around her house. It looks pretty good, we have quite a lot to sell.

Doors open in 5 minutes. Wish me luck! I'm ready to sell, sell, sell!

12.17

I haven't sold a single pair yet and it's getting pretty cold in here, standing around, drinking a lot of tea. I did have a mooch around earlier and managed to buy a really cool multicoloured, bobbly scarf, carrot cake jam for Jack and a vintage looking tunic all for £7.50. What a bargain! Booom! Definatley spending more than I am making though. It's ok. Technically I am contributing by giving other stalls money and raising money for charity.

Jack's Mum and her pals are so nice. Vicky, one of her close friends, has a granddaughter called Katie. When she see's me she runs across the room screaming 'ELISEEE'! And jumps into a hug.

Katie's fun, I have known her since she was about three. The first time I met her I was staying at Jack's and she came over early in the morning, ran upstairs, jumped on my bed and shouted 'Who are you? Your hair is a mess!' I hid my head under the covers until someone came to get her and apologised for the rude awakening. She's now 11 and a lot cooler.

13.34

I am just tucking into a hotdog when Brad texts me: *How's it going?*

Yeah! It's good... haven't sold a single thing BUT loving life.

You have to start somewhere and you are very determined and dedicated so you will get there.

I would like to do the world beer stall so might start looking into that soon. Jewellery is more of a hobby.

Once I played a gig to four people and thought it was so embarrassing but now, I'm playing at a festival with other bands so it's all worth it.

That's cool. You must love that! Well I'm just giving it a go and starting out but you are actually succeeding...but thank you for believing in me.

15.00

As I'm packing up, I started telling Katie all about List Life.

'That's cool! Can I give you a list?' She says, whilst eating the sweets her Nan has given her to keep her entertained.

'Ermm, yeah sure, but I have to be able to do it by this time tomorrow,' I explain.

When we are leaving, she comes over to me and hands me a pink note which reads:

Buy Popcorn

Sit down and relax

Watch a film

She said I'm very busy and need to take a break. Aww, bless her, but it's a list and it must be done!

15.45

I am not religious so not sure if I would be accepted but I would love to do this. Run activities and events to raise money to go to Sri Lanka. When they are out there, they help out in schools and hospitals and places like that but one day they treat all the children to a McDonalds. How cool is that? They all said it's their favourite day and the kids love it. A proper little treat for them all! The church is only up the road from me and I wonder if I could come here every Sunday? Maybe I might give it a go.

17.30

It's been such a nice day, chilling with Jan and her friends. She hasn't sold anything either but it's just been nice to be with genuinely nice people, doing something helpful for the community. And I've been invited to a quiz night in March. Social little bunch!

I text Jack to tell him we need to stay in and watch a film with popcorn tonight but he texts back saying that it's not a good idea on a Saturday because I will make it to 9 o'clock then end up in tears because I feel trapped, which is very true.

'Let's go to the cinema instead,' he suggests.

That's a much better plan and I can still relax, watch a film and eat popcorn. Perfect!

18.30

We're in Frankie and Benny's grabbing some early dinner before the film and I thought I would get Jack to choose my dinner for fun. At first, he seemed up for it but then he was looking at the menu debating between chicken pasta and a BBQ meat feast pizza and started getting so stressed saying he doesn't want to ruin my dinner.

'Why are you so worried? Just choose anything.' I am so confused.

'Because food is important to you and if I choose the wrong thing it will ruin your night.'

'Haha, don't be ridiculous! I will eat anything,' I laugh.

'OK but don't blame me if you don't like it!'

When the waitress comes over, he decides on the pizza. Bad choice! It came out and there was something spicy in it! Why does this kind of stuff make me so grumpy? I can't say anything to Jack because I was the one that told him to choose my dinner, but my face says a thousand words.

'Do you hate it? Oh, Elise I'm sorry this is why I don't do things like this. Do you want to swap?'

'No, it's ok. It's just that I'm hungry now and I can't eat it, it's actually hurting me!'

'What, the spice?' Sorry I didn't know it was going to be spicy. Look, have some of mine and we will get some popcorn when we get in.'

'Ok, thank you, sorry for making you choose.'

He just shakes his head and laughs. 'I told you it was a bad idea.'

23.20

Oh my god, that was another VERY bad idea! As I couldn't find a film that really interested me, I told Jack to choose and so he chose a film and God only knows what it was about but I had my hands over my face and fingers in my ears the whole time. It was horrible! People being graphically killed and dodgy drugs deals. It was awful! He has promised that, from now on, I will choose all films (and dinners).

Brad text saying he has been out with his pals and told them about List Life and now every time he does something Dave is says 'Is that because dominatrix told you to?'

Haha That's hilarious!

Even though the film and meal were rubbish, it was good to get out with Jack and have a proper 'Date night'. When we get in, I put on a stand-up comedy DVD to make up for the horrendous film. Turned out it was a good night in the end, not as relaxed as Katie would have liked me to have but it was nice.

11th February

10.00

I love Sunday mornings because we just sit and chat for an hour or so in the morning with our coffee, like American sitcom characters.

'Jack, list 10 things you are scared of.'

He answers straight away. 'I fear when I put the key in the door and realise I haven't told you about a game that's on TV and it's about to start.'

'Really? Good! You should warn me about stuff like that. What else?'

'Spiders I suppose. I mean, not exactly a fear but I don't like them. Oh, and when we go into places with fragile ornaments and you take your bag in there and I'm terrified you are going to smash something. Or, when we are on the motorway and we have passed the service station and you say you're hungry and I know it's about 10 miles to the next one.'

'So, I am your fear?'

'Ermm, yeah, I suppose so.' We both burst out laughing.

'I don't really have any phobias. Obviously, things like my own death and other people dying scares me but not heights or animals or anything. How about you?'

'Oh loads: Dogs, although seeing Casper the other day wasn't that bad, rides, spiders, but same as you, not like a full-on fear, public speaking, drugs, being attacked or abused, people dying and stuff like that.'

'What a mess,' he chokes.

'Oi!' I laugh, and throw a cushion at him. 'Right! Can we walk down to the high street? I want to get some knitting stuff and some food for the week. Oh…and a fish.' I say, then really quickly, jump up and run to get ready but he follows me into the room.

'Do we still have to do that?'

'You said you wanted to get a fish? Plus, we were meant to get one last week and forgot so need to get one today.'

'Yeah, I suppose we can. Ok I know a garden centre at the top of the high road. Let's go there after!'

I realise I haven't got a list today. Feels kind of empty but also kind of free.

12.03

We are half way to get the fish and I have changed my mind. I don't want a fish. You have to clean it out all the time and remember to feed it but Jack is actually excited and said it was part of the list so we have to do it. Oh, now he wants to join in, does he? Where was this attitude when I was asking him for a list?

'Where are we going to put it? The tank is on the kitchen side at the moment but we can't keep it there.'

'We can make some room on the shelving unit and it can go there. Stop worrying. It's only a fish,' he laughs.

We pull up to the garden centre and head in. There is a much bigger selection than the last one I went to. Massive ones, tiny ones, black, silver, red ones, even a multi-coloured one with a lobster in the tank. Maybe we can get one of those instead.

'How about this one?' Jack points at one that, to be fair, looks exactly like the one I chose before: A flamboyant diva, who suits the name 'Josh the Great.'

'Perfect!' I agree.

So, we get him and I hold him in his little bag all the way home. Do you remember getting them at the fair ground? Do they still do that?

When we arrive home, we set up the tank with fresh water and Jack finds him a spot on the shelving unit. Aww I quite like Josh the Great. Makes the flat look homely. Another one of list life's little miracles.

14.40

Sitting in my living room with my second cup of coffee, knitting and staring at Josh the Great. I quite like him actually, seems like a cool guy. I hope he is happy with his rock-shaped tunnel and fake seaweed.

I text Brad: *What's your band's name again? I know you told me the other day but I have forgotten.*

Twisted World. Why?

No reason… just wanted to have a listen.

Don't judge me.

Why would I judge you?

Because I don't want to be stereo-typed as a metal-head.

Just because you are in a metal band, doesn't mean you are a metal head. I love metal but I'm also listening to a bit of old-school gangsta rap, whilst sitting in my Moroccan style room, dressed in a Sex Pistols t-shirt, knitting! No-one can stereo-type me! Anyway, stereo-typing is sometimes a good thing.

So, you got your knitting then?

Yep, I had to watch a few YouTube videos to pick up the technique but I think I might be smashing it.

Check you out!

So, don't get angry with me, but I told my mate about Twisted World and she loves it! I knew she would. It's amazing! Are you excited about your gig?

Kind of...but I haven't heard from the guys in a while so not sure when the next practice will be.

Right, I need to get a list for tomorrow. I'm bored and Jack said he hasn't had a chance to write one yet. Have you asked your Mum to do one? She seems like someone who would be up for a laugh.

No, because I think it's your thing, and they might ruin the concept.

The concept is how you see it. Like, when I did Josh's it was hard. There were too many things on the list but I knew he was trying to stitch me up. I knew that I had to do it to prove something but actually, once I had done it I realised it pushed me to do things that I didn't know I could do. I was proud of myself for the things I had achieved and also that I hadn't looked stupid.

I hated him for doing that because it wasn't what is was all about and he used it to ruin it.

But, he didn't ruin it and that's the point. So, the next time you gave me a list, I knew it would be productive. I knew it wouldn't be a test and it was comforting. Ok this is now way too deep.

Yeah, you are sounding like a bit of a drip, but I know what you mean. Glad that's how you feel about my lists.

Talking of being productive, I've just remembered I need to apply for jobs. I can't stand that place!

I keep looking at jobs but then think it is good money so don't want to leave.

I know. I keep looking and realising they do pay well, probably because you wouldn't stay otherwise. Also, I really want to start my own thing up so think it might be safe to stay there while I do that so I'm a bit more secure.

Still thinking about the beer stall?

Yeah, I keep looking into it and think it's a really good idea.

Go for it! Like you say you have a secure job, Jack and your family to support you and you keep talking about it, so, give it a go!

Ahhh this is so hard. I don't know what to do and where to start.

I will make it easy for you. Find one job tonight to apply for, then make a list of 10 thing you need to research for a beer stall.

Oh my God! Yes! I can do this!

I flick my laptop open and write a list of things I need to do to start a beer stall:

Check how to get a personal license and the cost?

What would I use as a bar? Van? Adapted trailer?

What type of beer?

How much to stock?

Where can I keep the beer?

How to make profit?

What type of events?

How to promote?

Certificates needed?

Where can I get the beer?

Oh wow! This is so exciting I'm going to really look into this!

Thank you for helping me Brad!... I have written my list and I'm now researching beer and it's so exciting. Did you know the most sold beer in the world is 'Snow' lager? But it's only sold in China, they must drink a lot of it.

Wow really! That's a good fact and you know I love a fact! Haha, if you ever need help let me know. Also, I'm ok at researching (tasting) beer if you need any help? Pub?

Haha, that's true. I need to now research beer types and flavours. What a great plan to talk through over a pint!

18.05

I'm just getting into my research when my brother, Harvey texts: *What's all this about you doing some weird list game? Mum is raving about it to everyone.*

Is she? To who? I type with a massive smile on my face.

Nan, all her friends, what is it? Can I write you one or are you the only one that can write a list?

No course not, I can write one for you or you can write one for me. Wanna do it?

Yeah, but I will write you one. I'm not sure I want you to write me one yet. I am out at the moment but as soon as I get in, I will send you one.

Wooo! Harvey's on board, this will be a stitch up for sure! I can't wait.

I need to book the class for salsa on Thursday. How exciting!

20.10

We went out for dinner because it's the end of the weekend and couldn't think of anything else to do. Eating is always the answer. I will start my diet tomorrow and will make a salad to take to work with me.

I am having a break from making jewellery so we sit down and watch TV with bread and the chutney I bought from the fete on Saturday.

22.05

I hear my phone buzz but I can't remember where I put it last.

'It's on the radiator in the bedroom,' Jack says without looking up from the TV. I swear this guy knows everything. I lose my glasses, phone, keys, you name it, I lose it. Anyway, he must make mental notes when walking round the flat.

The text is from my brother and reads:

Wear two buns on each side of your head tomorrow at work.

Go to a park and go down the slide 3 times in a row (on your own)

Drink a cold cup of tea

Sing an Abba song and film it and send it to the family WhatsApp group

Beep at every blue car you see (only on the way to work)

Oh bejeez. They are going to think I am mad at work! Right I am going to practice the hair now! I'm thinking maybe the best way to do this is to do plaits then roll them into buns. That way they should stay up longer.

Plait on each side…easy

Roll into buns… harder but do-able

Trying to keep them there…Impossible

Why is hair the most difficult thing to do in the world? I have watched four YouTube videos and they make it look so easy. Immaculate girls with thick, long locks, rolling them up without a mirror and sliding bobby pins in without any difficulty. I am looking in the mirror and still keep sticking the pins in my hands or sliding them the wrong way because the reflection is backwards. Jack has been rolling his eyes at me the whole time and trying not to laugh in case he gets a death stare.

23.45

FINALLY, I have worked out how to do it and will have to get up uber early tomorrow morning to make sure I have enough time.

Chapter 11- This means business

12th February

My hair is looking on point! Getting up at 5.45am to master it was worth the struggle. Now I just need to wear something that is going to go with this bizarre-looking hair. I find the orange tunic I bought from the church fundraising day and the thick, multicoloured scarf. I think this might be way too hippy but who cares! I'm going to go for it. Nothing to lose at this stage. No-one there talks to me, let alone has any opinions on how I look.

07.00

On my way to work I have to drive through Epping forest, which in February, at 7am is pretty dark. It's quite a lonely, spooky drive at this time of the morning and there are hardly any cars around…apart from today. As I drive down the winding, pitch black, desolate roads of the forest, I see a car coming towards me and slow down so we can both pass without rolling down the bank and then I see it…it's a bright BLUE fiesta. Oh, good God, it's too early and too quiet for this but here goes BEEEEP!!!

The guy slows down and stares at me and then sticks his middle finger up. Calm down, I think to myself. I thought that was it but then he wound down the window and shouted 'Who do you think you're tooting at you fucking moron?!'

Oh no! Oh God! Please help! There are two men in the car and they are angry! I shouldn't have done this. I just shrug but that makes him even more mad. He hands something to the guy next to him and goes to open the door but then, thankfully, someone pulls up behind him so he throws a cup of half empty coffee at my car before speeding off. Thank God! I thought he was going to get out and murder me. Seriously, does tooting make people that angry. I'm a mess, that really freaked me out and I'm shaking.

Two minutes later I see another car coming my way and yes you guessed it, its blue! I don't want to do this but I can't fall at the first hurdle. So again, I toot but slightly hesitantly this time, it was quick and sharp. The lady driving the car jumped and then tooted back as if I was saying 'HI' and waved. Haha aww bless her, that made me laugh, maybe this tooting lark is fun.

Once I had made my way to the M25, it was easy. No one can hear anything on there and even if they did, by the time they realised what has happened, they were five cars away. I was pressing the horn as if I was a judge on X factor!

When I get to work, I drive to the car park and there are four blue cars. I have been so confident along the way here that as soon as I seen them. I toot four times. Bill comes running out in a panic!

'WHAT?!' He shouts. Oh shit!

'Oh…nothing. Sorry my brother told me to toot at all blue cars and there were four in here sooo…' I explain, sheepishly.

'Stop your stupid games Elise. Some people are trying to work!' he shouts, and goes back inside.

I can't contain my laughter. It's so funny. Why is he getting so angry?

It's only 8.30am so how much work is he doing? Most of the morning he is only letting people in that have forgotten their pass. I roll my eyes and rummage through my bag 'Oh shit!' I curse to myself, I am one of those people… oh lord he is going to FLIP!

10.50

After the dramas of this morning, it seems like a pretty standard day. Same old quiet office until…

'Nice Hair'

I turn around but everyone was tapping away at their keyboards. Kathy was on the phone, Tom was texting and looked deep in conversation. Who said that? I carry on typing and then I realise. It was Monika. What? I thought she didn't speak.

'Sorry, did you say you like my hair?' I ask.

'Yes,' she said in her very deep, Bulgarian accent, still not looking up from her desk. ‘It’s interesting.’

‘Oh thanks, yeah it took me ages to do. It was on a list from my brother. I spent ages last night trying to….’ I realise she has put a headphone back in her ear and zoned out ages ago. Oh, ok, no worries, I look up slightly embarrassed and making sure no one heard me and Brad is staring at me all sympathetic and mouths ‘Awww’

‘Ermm does anyone want any tea? I’m going to get tea,’ I quickly ask and hope no one says yes because I want to get out of the office.

‘Yeah, sure I’ll come with you! I want one of those bourbons,’ Tom says, oblivious to what I am trying to do.

11.00

Standing in the kitchen and Tom is telling me about how his new boyfriend is devastated because his budgie got murdered last night.

I choke on my tea. ‘MURDERED?!’

He looks so sad ‘Yes murdered…’ he repeats, whilst stirring his 25 sweeteners into his tea.

‘Oh my god Tom how? By who? Was he burgled?’

‘By the neighbour’s cat…Tilly.’

I throw my hand up to my mouth, trying to look like I am in shock but actually I don’t think I can contain my laughter. It’s not that it’s even funny. Of course not. It’s just that ‘murdered’ doesn’t seem the right word to use. I’m not sure, maybe it is. Maybe I’m just a horrible person.

As if to save this awkward moment, Jenny comes into the kitchen. Normally, she chats to Tom about crystals and ghosts and stuff but today she comes straight over to me and says 'Wow babe, I like your hair!' I look at her confused.

'Are you serious? It looks ridiculous, but my brother wrote me a list and one of the things on it was 'wear two buns on your head.'

'Oh yeah. Tom was telling me about your lists, it sounds good. He said Josh made you buy a fish?'

'Yeah, he did but when I went to get the fish, I had to have all the stuff for three days before I could get it. He is currently making himself at home in my little flat.'

'Such a cool idea. Maybe you can write me one, one day?'

'Yes sure!' How exciting! Everyone is getting involved.

13.30

Lunch time finally rolls round and when we get outside of the building, Brad lunges towards me with his arms out. I hate hugs so push him away but he just wraps his arms right round my folded arms.

'What are you doing?' I snap.

'Awww, I felt so sorry for you earlier with Monika.'

'Oh pfft, please, as if I care about her.' I tut.

'Did you give her a list the other day, when I said you should?'

'Well, yes, but only because I didn't know what to say to her.'

'No, it wasn't,' he laughs. 'It's because you didn't want her feeling nervous and wanted to break the ice. You're not as hard as you think you are, you know.'

'Ermm, excuse me!' I shout. 'I do *not* care actually and anyway it's only a game!'

'Ok ok,' he raises his hands in surrender. I pull a grumpy face at him and get in the car. I pretend to be pissed off with him and text Molly in order to ignore him, but as I'm texting her it comes to light that she only works 10 minutes round the corner from us. I get over my strop and tell Brad. We arrange to meet up tomorrow for a Chinese all-you can-eat buffet lunch. He has never met her and I have been trying to set them up, even though I don't think they suit really. Plus, I asked him today what his perfect date would be and he said: 'London Dungeons, followed by a drink in a quiet pub, then a walk to a station or a car park to drop her off…' Sounds like a horror film. Oh well, they're both single and you never know.

15.34

I am just texting Will, when Jonny comes in.

Jonny is one of the guys from the warehouse who I first met onsite at one of the jobs. I had only been at the company about a month and I was just standing there watching how they set everything up (I was only meant to be standing there, I wasn't just not working) I was starting to get hungry and wanted to leave but felt like I couldn't just say 'Well, bye then.' Then this short, Italian-looking guy came skipping over to me, smiling from ear to ear.

'Are you bored? If you have nothing to do there's an art gallery over the other side of the car park. I have 10 minutes before I have to do an equipment check. Wanna come over with me and have a look?'

'Yeah, sure, if they don't mind? I don't want to just run away.'

'Don't worry. See that guy over there?' He pointed to a tall, slightly larger, very angry-looking man. 'He's the manager and look how stressed he looks. It's not going well at the moment so he won't even notice.'

We went over to the gallery and admired all the paintings, while Jonny voiced what he thought each person in them was saying or thinking. It was very amusing and made me feel at ease. Once we finished, he said he would tell the manager that I had gone because I needed to get back for a meeting.

Anyway, I haven't seen Jonny since that day and, just as I am texting Will back, he came bounding in the office and saw my hair and shouted 'WOW look at you! How cool is that hair? You look like Princess Leia.' I must have looked confused because then he went on to explain that she was a character in Star Wars.

It's been such a crazy day. People I haven't really spoken to have been talking to me, just because of my hair. It's mad. Maybe I am starting to fit in here.

I'm buzzing and I can drive home without tooting anyone!

18.30

When I get in, I start to make noodle soup with chicken and chilli because I need to get skinny and healthy. Plus, its cheap.

19.45

I have been trying to talk Jack into going down to the park for the past 20 minutes. He said it's too cold and it's raining, which is true BUT it's List Life and I feel like I have failed if I don't do it. I don't know if he is really hard work or the most patient man in the world.

'Elise you hate the rain and we are 26 years old. I'm not even sure we are allowed in play grounds at this age.'

'Jack, its quarter to eight, no one is going to see us and we can just go there. I'll go down the slide and then we will come home.'

'Ok, ok, go on then!' He finally gives in.

'Thank you, thank you!' I hug him and give him a peck on the cheek. 'Write me a list when we get back and I will do whatever you put on there tomorrow, and it can even be disown your brother, haha.'

'I like Harvey. It's you I'm going to disown! Now, come on you nutter. I want to watch the highlights at 10.30pm.'

I run and get my coat on and we run downstairs.

He's right. It's chucking it down and it's horrible.

He looks at me 'You don't want to go now do you?'

I shake my head and bite my lip.

He laughs, 'Thank god for that! Anyway, don't you have to sing along to Abba or something? I'll film you doing that instead.'

As soon as I get in, I run to the laptop and type 'Abba song with lyrics.' In the search engine. Waterloo is the first song that pops up so I go for it. Jack is filming me on my phone:

'Waterloo, couldn't escape if I wanted to…Waterloo knowing my fate is to be with you…. Woah woah woah woah…'

I'm half way though Jack asks, 'Shall I start filming yet?'

'WHAT!' I turn and look at him in disgust and he bursts out laughing 'I'm joking! I'm Joking!' he laughs and I carry on singing.

When I have finished, I send the video to my family WhatsApp group and they send me laughing emoji's and loads of 'HAAAAHHAHAHAHAHAHs'. Turns out I am an awful singer but it was very funny.

20.45

Trying to find a holiday to Portugal and it's driving me mad. Normally I think of a country, Google all the best places to go and choose one, but Portugal seems so hard! There are loads of places: Algarve, Porto, Albufeira, Lagos. How do I choose? They all say they are good. We just want a sun holiday with bars, restaurants, a pool and near to the sea. Not too much to ask.

Arghh! Why am I so stressed about this? I normally find a holiday straightaway and I love looking for good deals but this is proving difficult.

10.49

I got too stressed and now I am sitting on the sofa, seething and Jack has taken over. He never sorts the holidays out. I planned our whole six-month travel trip a few years ago. He just turned up. It's not that he refuses to do it. It's that I normally love it.

I did text Brad to see if he has been and he just mentioned all the places I'd already heard of but he said there isn't a place that is particularly best and that they are all good.

He then changes the conversation, probably because I sound mad.

Question: When I asked you at lunch the other day about your beer stall venture, what was the other idea you had? I was trying to think of it earlier.

It's to organise an event where people come and bring food from their own culture. I grunt but it's on text so he can't hear the tone.

Oh yeah, I remember now! I've got a few ideas you can do for that if you want to run through them tomorrow?

Yeah ok sure.' I type and then slump back into the sofa. I grab the chocolate bar I was eating earlier and sulk.

Then I had a genius idea!

'Jack, you know the beer stall idea and the cultural dish event, I keep talking about?'

'Yeah?' He is still in deep concentration, looking for a holiday.

'Do you think I should ask Brad if he wants to help me do it?'

'Yeah that's a good idea. He's into that sort of thing too, isn't he? Plus, you can both put money in and make it amazing!'

'Oh yeah! I didn't think of that! Ooo I will ask him!'

I scramble for my phone and text Brad back.

So, I was just speaking to Jack and came up with an idea...

Oh God not another one. Too many business plans! Stick to one! Haha

No, funny boy. Would you be interested in doing the event with me and it can be our event?

He doesn't text back for ages and I am starting to get nervous that he is thinking of all the different excuses he can give. Then my phone finally buzzes:

Are you serious?! YES of course, how cool would that be? Also, I have loads of ideas. Wait, are you sure?

Yeah, course! It will be fun, plus I was just speaking to Jack and we can both put money in so it makes it a better event.

Yeah definitely. We can add music. I'll tell you what I mean tomorrow.

So, he has been thinking about this already.
Oh my God! This is so amazing! Imagine if my dream of my own business actually does come true!

Well we can do this event and then you can use the profits to start up your beer stall.

Yes! Let's do this!

Meanwhile, while I am making business plans, Jack as smashed the holiday search and we have booked a week away in Portugal in July…I am so excited! Best night ever!

22.30

As Jack is now watching the highlights and I am waiting for my tea to turn cold, I thought I would start getting ready for bed. I take my hair out of the buns and it is WILD! I have quite straight hair normally and as I have mentioned before it is very orange so it looks mental! It does kind of look cool though.

I get into my fleece, leopard print pj's and sit down with Jack to drink my horrendous tea. It's like drinking dish water and it got me thinking… who invented tea? I mean, who said we are going to boil up some leaves and then, when it is boiling hot, add some cold milk until it goes a light brown colour. In all honesty it sounds vile and here I am making it even more vile.

Right, done! Finally. That list was fun, funny but also a proper stitch up. Well done Harvey!

Buenas Noches!!! I found a website that also teaches Spanish so I'm keeping it up so far.

Chapter 12- This could end in tears

13th February

14.33

Lunch was so cool! We set up in a café and made a business plan. We researched venues in London to host the event and listed ways to make it profitable but also fun! I am buzzing, I can't wait to build my little empire, step by step.

21.45

Nothing to report on during the day but tonight, I have been to see my pals from uni. We hardly ever meet up but it's always a good night when we do. Every time we meet, they each have a crazy story to tell.

Gemma has had a row with Gary, she chucked him out and burnt all of his clothes (don't ask).

Kelly is recently married but says that she is now debating whether she still likes the guy after their honeymoon. Apparently, he was flirting with one of the waitresses and she found an earring in his car when they got back. I've never trusted him to be fair.

Chanel is doing a second degree but has a seven-year-old daughter so is struggling with time and money. She's a super woman so she'll get through it.

I never have any stories. I've been with the same guy for eight years and he's the guy I met at Uni so they all know him really well. The only thing that they were all really interested in was List Life!

I've told them all about the things I have been up to and Gemma says 'Oh this is gold. We have to do you one.'

Shit, that's not good. These girls are vicious and will do anything to make me look as ridiculous as possible.

As soon as I am home, I turn off the engine and check my phone. I have three messages from the girls:

Gemma – *Drive to work with just your bra on the top half!*

Kelly – *Make naughty cupcakes*

Chanel – *Draw on thick, black eyebrows to work*

Gemma – *Text the 11th person on your phone contacts and say*

'Hey Gorgeous, I dreamt about you last night.'

Chanel – *Sign one of your work emails off with – Kind regards Bitch face*

Told you it would be a stitch up. Might not tell Brad because he said the other day that he hates it when people try and stitch me up with it. I can't be bothered with the drama.

14th February

06.30

I wake up and kiss Jack on the head 'Happy Valentines' and give him a DVD about The Kray Twins. I know it's not romantic but you must know me by now. Do I strike you as the romantic type?

He rolls over and attempts to open his eyes. 'Did you actually do Valentines this year?' He looks confused.

'Well, I didn't get one of those mushy cards but I got you a present because I'm out tonight.'

'Well I got you a typical 'Valentines' present' and he hands me a box of chocolates. 'But if you look in the bag in the fridge, I also got you and 'Elise' Valentines present.'

I jump out of bed and run to the fridge. There's a small gift bag in there. I look inside and there is a twin pack of massive scotch eggs! Yes! I love scotch eggs. In fact, I love anything savoury.

'THANK YOU!' I shout and I can hear him laughing to himself

in the bedroom, before he heads off to the bathroom for a shower.

07.00

The only bra that's clean is my bright red one. Oh, wow, I hope I don't get caught and arrested. Luckily it is 7am and dark outside. I refuse to walk to the car without a top on. It's too cold and I'm not that brave.

I get in the car and whack the heating on full blast. I will drive half way down the road and then pull over to take my top off. Is this illegal? Too late now I'm invested or un-vested, depending how you want to look at it.

I chose to drive the Mazda so that I am lower than the rest of the cars and hopefully, people will be too tired this time of the morning to even notice. Right tops off. I take a quick selfie to prove that I am doing it and send it to the girls. Now I'm off.

07.15

So far, I haven't seen one car because I am driving down the forest roads so there aren't many cars yet. Imagine if I see my angry friend again! Oh god I hope he isn't about, I can't be dealing with that this morning.

When I hit the main road leading up to the motorway there is huge queue of traffic. Oh please, don't do this to me!

As I drive up to the junction, a lady in a people carrier is letting me out but is also shouting at her kids in the back of the car so I whip out quick and no one sees me. Phew!

I finally get on the M25 and pick up enough speed so that no one notices me. Even if they have, I can’t see their reaction. This isn’t that bad actually, I mean, I don’t think anyone has even noticed. I turn the radio on and belt out some old school classics.

I spoke too soon! Up ahead there are orange lights on the road signs saying SLOW…TRAFFIC UP AHEAD! Oh, good Lord! I brake slowly, I really need the least time in this queue as possible but it comes to a stand-still. This is not good. I just need to concentrate on the road ahead and try to not make eye contact with any cars. I pull up next to a pick-up truck and can feel them pointing and laughing. It is causing such a commotion. I can’t help myself, I look up and they are crying with laughter, pointing and whistling. I am now as red as my bra. They suddenly stop and start looking down at their laps. Then, I realise they are sorting their cameras out on their phone. I am panicking so much, sweating and mouthing ‘Please don’t, please!’

Then, as if someone heard my cry, the traffic starts to move and I speed off. Oh God, this is the worst! I have a headache from the stress. I pull into the slow lane so there is less chance of being seen and turn up the music to cheer myself up.

7.45

I’m almost off the motorway when I get caught! Are you kidding me?! Ahhh, this is so mortifying and scary! I can see the flashing police lights in the rear-view mirror but where do you pull over on the motorway? The lights are flashing brighter. I start to pull over on the hard shoulder and scramble for my top. How is this happening. Is there a fine for this? Is it even illegal?

Once I have pulled over, I look back and there is no sigh of a police car behind me. I am now on the hard shoulder in a very shaded part of the road. Did I imagine it? Am I going mad? Then a cloud must have moved because the light hit my hair and it's so bright that it makes me squint. That's when I realise. It wasn't police lights flashing me, it was the light from the rising sun, hitting my bright orange head and making a flashing notion in the mirror. My body instantly relaxes and I start laughing uncontrollably. How ridiculous, I am now sitting on the hard shoulder for no reason laughing to myself. Luckily my top is now back on, otherwise passing traffic would have definitely reported me anyway. Oh God, how do I get back onto the road? What a journey this has been.

The rest of the drive was a lot calmer and thank God I didn't turn up to work without my top on, I would have definitely been reported to 'Higher Management' then, for sure.

When I get into the building, I head straight to the bathroom and straighten out my clothes, brush my hair and get my makeup bag out (which I don't normally bring to work by the way). I usually sketch on a light brown eyebrow pencil before I leave the flat as my eyebrows are really blonde.

I don't have a black eyebrow pencil so I use the eyeliner. I start shading them slightly to get the right shape and then I layer it on thick. It looks ridiculous. I am ginger with thick, black eyebrows! I look terrifying. Thank God I am not customer-facing today.

When I walk through the door Tom cannot control himself. He is laughing so much that he's struggling to breathe. Luckily Kathy isn't in yet so I feel like I can explain without being told to be quiet. Monika is in early but as per usual doesn't say a word.

As I head to my desk, I bump into Jonny again. He looks at me oddly 'Please tell me that is on one of your lists and you do not think that looks good?'

'I don't think what looks good?' I try and act oblivious.

'Why are your eyebrows black?'

'Ohhh that! Yeah, I had them dyed last night, do you like them?' I chirp, still keeping up the act.

'Do you have to wash it off and then it goes lighter?'

'No, I asked for black because my eyebrows are normally blonde so it will save on makeup.'

'Oh, I see! Yeah, makes sense. Looks amazing!' He changes his tone to sound positive.

'I'm joking Jonny, of course it's on my list! It looks horrendous doesn't it?'

He breathes out a sign of relief as if he has been holding his breath for a decade.

'Oh, thank God. It looks so bad! Who gave you that one?'

'My pals. They are bitches but it's fine. People here know about the lists anyway.'

09.00

Brad is late as usual. I have warned him about the eyebrows before-hand to avoid any embarrassment but it doesn't help. As soon as he sits down, he bursts out laughing.

'It's so bad Elise, sorry but it looks awful.' I ended up telling him about the list in the end because I knew I would look like this today.

'Thanks mate,' I roll my eyes and half smile.

Bill, who as I have mentioned sits directly opposite me and has not mentioned the monstrosity on my face yet, suddenly says 'I thought you looked a bit odd today but just thought you had done your hair differently like yesterday.'

'Bill my eyebrows are BLACK! Anyway, what's wrong with my hair?' I snap. He just shrugs and carries on with his work.

Kathy, who has yet again, only got herself a tea, comes back to her desk and grunts say 'Attention seeking again are we Elise?'

I start to laugh to myself and quickly text Brad: *Is she for real? Did you see her flirting at 80 decibels yesterday with Harry Carter down the phone, flicking her hair about like a wild pony?*

What a joker!

11.00

Right, I need to crack on with this list. I scroll down to the 11th person on my contacts list, I count them as I scroll down 1,2,3,4,5,6,7,8,9,10,11…NO!

I put phone down and place my head in my hands. I can't do it! It's too weird. The 11th contact is Alfie! Jack's brother! Oh God! This is a nightmare. I have known Alfie since day one of knowing Jack, he's like a brother, oh no what am I going to do?

11.12

Hey Gorgeous, I dreamt about you last night.

I have been hovering over the send button for 10 minutes, I can't bring myself to do it.

'Smith! You still doing that stupid list thing?' Someone shouts from behind me.

I turn around and Josh is in the office with Aaron and two other guys from the warehouse. They're all laughing and talking about me not being able to get a fish that day and saying 'I doubt she even got one anyway. She's all talk, that one.'

I grab my phone and hit 'send' then march over.

'I did get a fish actually! I got him on Saturday!' I show them all a photo of 'Josh the Great' that I have saved on my phone. 'I haven't failed a single task yet,' I lie, because I didn't go down the slide on my brother's list but I have done well and I'm not having these prats make me out the fool.

'Ooo, alright! Calm down I'm only messing around,' Aaron laughs.

I look him up and down 'Your flies are undone.' I point out and strut off like I dropped the mic. I can hear them all laughing at him as I walk off and smile to myself. Arsehole!

14.45

This afternoon, I have been training Monika on sending the equipment but she's always so blunt. Only one-word answers, it drives me mad, so I decide to see if she wants to chit chat.

'You up to much tonight?'

'Going out.' She replies.

'Ooo where? Anywhere nice? With your boyfriend?'

'Just out. Do I have to click this button to send the quote?'

See, she always cuts me off. What is her problem?

I answer, then turn away to carry on with my emails. One comes in, enquiring about some speakers from a supplier I don't recognise, so I reply:

Good afternoon Mr Gomez,

Thank you for enquiring with us today.

In order to provide you with the correct equipment for your event, please can you confirm the following information:

Nature of the event eg: Music, sporting, conference etc

Expected capacity

Venue type

Date and time frame of the hire

If you have any further queries please do not hesitate to contact us.

Kind regards

Bitch Face

…SEND

It's risky, but I have a plan. If anyone asks, I will deny any knowledge that I have sent the email and maybe blame it on autocorrect. I mean auto-correct has got me in many difficult situations in the past, with words that don't even remotely look like what I was meant to send, so I'm sure they can except Elise Smith has been changed to Bitch Face. I'm going to get a cup of tea. I feel all grumpy.

16.30

The rest of the day has been pretty average really nothing to report on. Brad asked if I could give him a list but I said, instead of writing him a list, I think he should redesign his flat to make it *his* flat, not his and his ex-wife's flat. He keeps saying things remind him of her, not that he misses her, but just that he didn't have control of his life when they were together. I mean I don't know her and have only met her that one time in the pub, so there is no way I can judge but, by knowing Brad, she probably only had control because he doesn't like making decisions.

17.00

Will had to cancel our previous plans because his meeting rescheduled so we are going out tonight instead. I warned him we have to go to salsa and he seems pretty up for it. I text the others and we have made plans to meet up in town next to the bar where it's being held. I haven't told the others that Will is coming yet, so it will be a nice little surprise for them. Will has moved all over the place since we left school but now lives in Brighton. I can't wait to see them all!

18.30

We have been on the phone for 10 minutes trying to locate each other. When I see him come around the corner, he hangs up and we scream and run towards each other.

We walk down to the bar and I tell him that I haven't told the others that he is coming so they might go crazy.

We turn around the corner and see Natalie, Graham, Louise and Tanya waiting for me to arrive. They spot me but they are all squinting trying to work out who I am with and then all at the same time, they clock it's Will and start bouncing around like excited puppies. It's so nice to see him and all be back together again.

This wouldn't have happened if Josh hadn't put it on my list! So, thank you Josh, even though it was meant to be a joke. It all worked out pretty nicely. Also, Brad told me to make a plan so salsa was one of the plans.

19.00

Standing around waiting for the teacher to set up her speakers and there seems to be a real buzz in the room. There are about 10 people waiting for the class, some in pairs, some on their own. You can tell who has been coming here for a while and who are the newbies.

'I feel quite nervous' Will whispers to me, 'Everyone seems to know what they are doing.'

'I know but I'm sure we will pick it up. Anyway, it's only a laugh.'

'It's fine, I've done this load of times,' Tanya boasts. 'I used to be a dancer.'

'When? We have known you most of your life and I've never known you to be a dancer?' Graham voices what we are all thinking.

'When we were at school I used to dance, just didn't tell you guys! I was in shows and everything,' she flicks her hair and purses her lips.

Natalie looks at her and shakes her head laughing, 'Course you did Tan.'

'RIGHT! Are we ready for some salsa?' The teacher shouts and then the music starts. 'Follow me, this is only a warm up so don't worry if you are unable to do the steps straight away.'

We all shuffle to an area where we can see her but stay nearer the back so we're not in the spotlight. Tanya has made her way to the front and is practically standing with the professionals.

This is hilarious. We are all over the place (Tanya included). I have tripped over my own feet three times. Natalie keeps looking back and laughing.

I am just starting to get the hang of it when the door opens and a cold breeze travels across the room. I would not like to turn up late to this. It's so embarrassing. I turn and look towards the door and a young girl sneaks in and apologises. She takes off her scarf and I look back to the teacher because I am missing the next step. Wait! I fling my head over my shoulder to double take…It's Monika!

She sits on a seat at the back of the class and changes into some different shoes, then joins in.

After a couple of minutes, she catches my eye and smiles. Wow, I didn't know she did salsa. This is something she could have mentioned. Anyway, I look forward and concentrate on the teacher, who has now stopped the warm up and is dividing us into groups based on experience. Obviously, we are all in the beginners' class but I'm surprised to know that Monika is too.

20.30

The class is so much fun. A little bit weird at first because you have to dance with random men but after the initial awkwardness, it's fine. Graham, Louise and Natalie love it and say they want to do it every week. Tanya said it seems a bit basic and that she might try to find a class that suits her level, hahahaha.

We are all buzzing and chatting away, then I see Monika on her own.

'Guys, I'm just going to speak to that girl over there, I work with her so should go and say hi!'

'Sure,' they all sing in unison.

As I approach her, she looks up and smiles 'Hi!' she chirps. 'I didn't know you came to salsa?'

'It's our first time, as you could probably tell,' I laugh. 'How about you? How long have you been doing it?'

'Oh, this is only my second week, I did an online salsa lesson as part of the list you gave me and loved it so thought I'd give it a go because it's hard without a partner.'

'The list?' I can't help sounding surprised.

'Yeah, you gave me a list last week, remember?' She looks confused.

'Yeah, I remember. I just didn't think you had done it.'

'Yeah actually that's why I wasn't in for a few days after. I was telling Ivo, my boyfriend about it when I got home and he said we should go out for a seafood platter as the 'Posh meal' but I got a severe allergic reaction from the crab and ended up in hospital.' She's laughing about it but, woah, that wasn't what was meant to happen.

'Oh my God! Are you ok? I'm so sorry!'

'No, I'm fine. They just gave me some tablets and I recovered quite quickly. I had to have a few days off for it to calm down, plus that place is so boring. What is Kathy's problem?'

'What?! I thought you liked her and that you hated me?'

'No way! I just don't speak because I know how she reacts around you and I need to keep a low profile if I want to keep the job.'

'That's true! She is crazy! So, did you do any more of your list?'

'Yeah, I have nearly finished the portrait so I will bring it in tomorrow maybe, but there's one I have done but I feel so bad about it and I'm not sure what to do.'

'Go on…?' I'm intrigued.

'The person I text that I haven't in ages is my ex and we have been texting ever since and he wants to meet me for a drink tonight after this.'

'Wow, ermm, well I don't know your boyfriend or ex so you gotta do, what you gotta do.'

'I think I might just go and see what he has to say, I do really miss him but Ivo is a really nice guy. Well, I'll let you get on because it looks like your mates are waiting for you. I'll see you tomorrow at work.'

We say our goodbyes and I head out with the others. That's was such a surreal experience. She is actually a really nice girl and she is doing the list! This is crazy! Right after all that dancing and drama I'm hungry.

20.45

We head to Annie's diner for dessert. I have updated them on the goss and now we are talking about my birthday on the 22nd April and deciding how to celebrate.

'What day is it this year?' Graham asks.

'Let me check.' Tanya grabs her phone. 'It's a Saturday and it says *Earth Day* in my calendar as a national day.'

'How odd, it says that in my calendar too? I have never noticed that before. What is it?'

Louise, who has been researching the whole time says, 'Earth Day is an annual event celebrated around the world on April 22 to demonstrate support for environmental protection apparently.'

'That's weird, I have never heard of it and I always check the calendar to see when my birthday is.'

There is silence as we are all reading about it, then I suddenly have an idea!

'Guys! Because its Earth Day, why don't I have a party at the flat with an Earth day theme, so we all have to dress as something related?'

'Like what? Pollution?' Natalie add sarcastically.

'No, like nature or erm, something to do with recycling?'

'Oooo, I could come as Eve and you could come as Adam, Graham!' Tanya starts laughing.

'Actually, this is a really good idea!' Graham announces.

'Wooo, lets, do this! I will invite loads of people and we can all do it,' I'm so excited.

We spend the rest of the night searching for fancy-dress ideas and talking about how we could make it eco-friendly.

22.00

When I get home, I check in with Brad to see how he is getting on with the flat.

Thank you Elise, I think I needed to do this. I always wanted a music corner to set my keyboard up and now I have ordered a desk from Ikea and am going to pick it up at the weekend. I have moved the dining room table into the spare room because I don't eat there on my own. I might make that room into an office for us to work in if we need to do any office work for this event.

That's a great idea! So glad you are making it your own. Don't get rid of any of her stuff or memories though because one day you might not feel like you do and it might be a nice memory.

I have put most of it in a cupboard or under the bed so it's out of the way. Tomorrow, when we go to lunch, can you come with me to help me find a new duvet cover? At the moment its purple with some sort of flowery pattern.

Yes, but only if it's your decision. Don't ask me what I think because it has to be your flat.

Ok, ok I promise. This has knackered me out so I am going to bed.

Night. Oh Brad! Can you write me a list of stuff I need to research or do for this business tomorrow please? Just so it gets me started.

Sure, Night!

I jump on the sofa and lay on Jack's shoulder. 'S'up girl! You alright? Have fun with your pals?' He asks and wraps me in his arms and kisses the top of my head.

I tell him all about my night, about Monika, Earth day and my birthday plans and that Will made an appearance tonight.

'Jack can you please do me a list? I will do it tomorrow.'

'I don't know what to put on it, anyway you have loads of people doing it, you don't need me to do one.'

'I *do* need you to do one. Just put anything on it, whatever you want me to do.'

'I don't want you to do anything though. Just do what you're doing, it's your thing.'

'But it's a game and you won't join in.' I'm not annoyed but I don't understand why he won't get involved, everyone else has.

Even my Nan and Kathy have joined in.

'It's not a game though. You are doing things you want to do and achieving things.' He sounds so uninterested, it's like he thinks I'm a kid. His phone buzzes and he takes his arm from around me and takes it out of his pocket to read. How rude! We're having a conversation and I'm so pissed off!

I'm going to bed early. Why won't he join in? I slump on the bed and feel my eyes filling up.

After a few minutes he follows me in and I think it's because he knows I'm upset. But I'm wrong.

'El, did you text my brother today saying you had a dream about him?' He is frowning and looks confused.

SHIT! I forgot about that. I fling my head back onto the pillow in exhaustion.'Yes, I did. Gemma said I had to text the 11th person on my contacts list telling them I had a dream about them and my 11th contact was Alfie.'

'Hey Gorgeous?' He questions. Oh, good God, this is not the right time for this.

'Yeah, I had to add that too. Is he annoyed?'

'No, but he's asking if it was meant for someone else and is giving me the heads up.'

Oh shit, this is not good.

'Well, tell him it was on a list and that I was only messing around. As if I would do that.'

'El, I know this is all a laugh but now Alfie thinks you're having an affair.'

I run my fingers through my hair and start crying. I can't help it, I'm knackered and I feel let down by him.

'What's up El?' he questions as if he wasn't part of the conversation seconds ago.

'I just feel like everyone is getting involved in List Life but you don't want to be part of it. Now you and Alfie hate me.'

'We don't hate you. It's just you want to do EVERTHING on the lists and some people are putting things on there to take the piss.'

'No, they don't!' I know I sound defensive. 'Everyone thinks it's great, Brad, Nan, all my friends, even Katy gave me a list.'

'To be fair, she saw it as an opportunity to stich you up.'

'I know but it was fun and I just wish you would do one so we can both have fun with it. At the moment other people are doing them and so I'm focused on them and we don't do things together. If you do one, you would be in control of what I do that day!'

'I don't want to be in control! Why would I want to control you?!' he shouts.

I sigh and get into bed (after I have cleaned my teeth and taken my makeup off).

'Sorry Elise, I just don't know what to put on it. You do loads of stuff and you don't need me to tell you want to do. I'm rubbish at things like that and I don't want you to sit in and watch football with me if you don't want to, it will make you unhappy and bored.'

'Then why don't you give me challenges or fun things to do?'

'I just think you do all that yourself. You are always doing things and making people happy.'

'No Jack! That's a just a cop out. You can't be bothered!' I shout.

'Elise! It's not that! It's just that I can't think of anything and you seem so happy when you do them. What if I do one you can't do?'

'Thanks Jack, you have such little faith in me!' I'm a blubbering mess.

'Don't be ridiculous, it's not like that!'

'I've had enough! I'm moving back to Mum's tomorrow' I cry.

'Please don't say that. This is crazy!' he begs.

'I can't live here if we don't do things together. We do everything separately.'

'But you like that, I do that so you can do you own thing! I'll try to do you one for the weekend.'

'No you won't! You have been saying that for weeks, I've had enough. It's over!'

'Fine' he snaps and rolls over to sleep.

I cry into my pillow until I am knackered and can't cry anymore and then attempt to go to sleep.

Chapter 13- The realisation

9th February

06.00

What a horrible night. What a horrible morning. I feel so sad and shaky. My eyes are tiny, red and sore. I didn't sleep at all.

It's over! My whole eight years with Jack are over and all because of my stupid List Life! Why wouldn't he just do it? Why didn't he back down sooner so it didn't get this far? Maybe he wanted it to go this far. Maybe he realised living with me was too much and he finally saw a way out.

07.12

I have a shower, get dressed and I'm out of the flat as soon as possible. Jack didn't speak to me at all. This hurts so much. I call my Mum; I know it's early but I want to speak to someone on my side. I explain the fight, the way he didn't care and how we are over.

'Elise that's mad! I understand what you are saying but Jack is a really nice guy and he is extremely tolerant of the way you are. There is no reason to end it because of a silly game you are playing.'

'What!' I snap. That was not the reaction I was hoping for.

'No, sorry. What I am saying is that the lists are amazing. You have done so well and the world is catching on but Jack doesn't want to control you. He has no interest in stitching you up. I actually think he is taking it seriously and thinks you are doing really well with it. Dad and I were talking the other night and we're so proud of you for List Life. You are taking yourself out of your comfort zone, trying new things every day and encouraging others to do the same.'

'Exactly! So why doesn't he want to do it with me?'

'Because he has been with you a long time and he knows you have your things and he has his things and that's how you work. He respects you a lot and he probably secretly likes the fact that you doing these things but doesn't want to write you a list in case he gets it wrong or makes you feel uncomfortable.'

To be fair that is exactly what he said. Maybe he's just being the easy-going Jack everyone knows and loves rather than this kill-joy Jack I have created in my head.

I don't want it to end. I especially don't want it to be because of

List Life. What do I do now? Do I text him? Maybe I should leave it for now and see how I feel later.

08.45

I pull up in the car park, and sigh. This is not somewhere I want to be today. I don't have a girlfriend I can go and talk to about it all. I just feel sad.

I slowly walk through the office and when I get to my desk there is a note that reads:

Please see me in meeting room one as soon as you arrive.

It doesn't even say who it's from. Hmm, I take off my coat, straighten out my top and head to meeting room one but no one is there. I take a seat just in case it's an 'All company meeting' and I can look like the eager beaver.

I'm just scrolling through Facebook on my phone when the door opens and in walks Barry and Kathy with their laptops in hand.

'Morning!' I chirp, but they have really straight faces as if they are about to tell some BIG news.

'Elise, you've been called in this morning because we have received a very serious complaint.' Barry starts, without any pleasantries. Kathy is sitting back in her chair, arms folded, raised eyebrows and pursed lips.

'Complaint?! About me?' I imagine I look confused because I thought I got on with all the suppliers. Ok, they aren't what I call mates but we have a laugh.

'Yes, the complaint came from Mr Peter Gomez, regarding an email he received yesterday.' He looks so stern but his voice is calm.

Peter Gomez? I don't know a Peter Gomez… OH FUCK! I feel my face burning instantly and I know I am now bright red.

Right poker face, I can do this.

'Oh yes Mr Gomez, he enquired about some speakers I believe.' I try and sound posh to put them off scent. 'Yes, that's right, he asked if he could hire them for an event later on in the year. Do we not own those speakers? Is that the issue?'

'Elise you know what the issue is!' Kathy leans forward and taps the table with her finger.

'Sorry, I'm confused. What have I done?'

'Let me reiterate what Mr Gomez has said in his email:

Dear Sir or Madam,

I am writing to you to bring to your attention the fact that I am not satisfied with the level of customer service I received earlier on today from one of your employees.

I emailed enquiring about hiring a number of speakers for a large-scale, music festival I am hosting in September. I received an almost instant response from Elise Smith asking the usual questions. However, I was outraged to find that the email was signed not by Elise Smith, but from Bitch Face.'

My whole face burst with laughter, I can't help it. He has worded it in such a funny way, I have no idea how Barry and Kathy are sitting there with no emotion.

'I'm sorry, I'm so sorry it's just that obviously I didn't write Bitch face. Why would I sign a company email from Bitch face, it doesn't even make sense.' I'm still laughing but trying not to show it.

He waits for me to finish and carries on:

'*I understand this is not the level of customer service you, as a company pride yourself on and I would like this letter of complaint to be taken seriously.*

Please can you also provide me with a quote for the following...

Now, I don't know what this list game is your playing but it needs to stop.'

'But!' I interrupt 'I honestly didn't write that! It must have auto-corrected it.'

'To Bitch face?' Kathy is pulling an 'as if' face.

'Listen, I'm not sure how it happened and I am genuinely sorry but this isn't something I've done intentionally. Please let me know what I need to do now and I will put it right.' I beg.

'Well you do sound sincere and I very much doubt you would have gone to these lengths, so I am having a meeting later this afternoon about it and we will resume at the end of the day.' He closes his notepad and signals for me to leave.

I leave the meeting room and head to the toilets. As soon as I know there is no one else in there, tears stream from my eyes. No boyfriend and now potentially no job. What a mess. I want to text

Jack but he hates me. I just need to get through to lunch and then I will talk to Brad.

13.30

'WHAT!' Brad has hands in his hair looking shocked. 'Elise it's meant to be fun! It started off as a way of getting me up and doing things. You can't let it ruin your relationship! Jeeez! This is why I am staying single for a while. You lot are crazy!'

I am just staring at him. I was on the edge of tears when I told him, but this conversation has been a roller-coaster of emotions. First, I was going to have a meltdown then he made me furious. Now I am I'm laughing hysterically!

'Oi! Don't tar us all with the same brush.' I punch him on the arm and then fall back into the car seat. 'Oh God Brad! What am I going to do? I ended it over a list!'

'Well technically not even over a list,' he jabs.

'Oh help me! What am I going to do?' I sigh.

'Elise, don't be a drip. Text him! He's your boyfriend… you've been together eight years. Sort yourself out!'

Well that told me. I feel so stupid, maybe I am being over dramatic.

14.30

When I get back to the office, I text Jack: *Jack I'm so sorry. Forget the lists! I really don't want us to end, I will move my stuff to my Mum's if you really want, but I think, if we just talk about it tonight, we can work it out. Sorry again.*

I get a text back straight away:

Were you serious about moving out? I thought that was a joke? Forget the fight we are stronger than that! Oh, guess what? One of the guys from work has just come back from India with some really cool sweets you would like. I'll bring some back tonight. Love you, you melt x

What?! I was serious. Did he think that the whole thing last night was a joke? Elise this is what you wanted. Why are you going to cause another argument? I breathe in deep and text back:

Can't wait, see you tonight x.

If he has forgotten it, then I need to forget it too. No point in worrying about it. Now that's sorted I just have to save my job.

16.30

My hands are fidgeting in my lap, I'm so nervous. What if I get sacked and I can't afford China. This is a nightmare.

I can see Barry and Kathy talking outside the meeting room. They need to hurry up I finish at five. Actually, this could be my last ever half an hour. Technically if I get fired I could go travelling, Oo, or I could really give the beer stall venture a proper chance. Or I could make something and sell it from home, maybe an online jewellery business. Do I even need this job? This might be the best thing that happened to me, starting from fresh. A new slate. The world is my oyster. List life could take me anywhere.

My train of thought is interrupted by the click of the door opening.

'Right, Elise…' He takes a deep breath.

Here goes…

'We have been in discussions with management and we have decided to give you another chance.'

Hmmm…

'We have spoken to a number of our suppliers and they say that they have never had any issues. However, we do have some requests and we need you to cooperate,' he says with a smile.

'Sure,' I nod.

'Now, Kathy has suggested that we give you the requirements in the form of a list because apparently that's how you get things done.'

I look at Kathy and she is smiling at me and winks. Wow, maybe she doesn't think this whole thing is mad and just wants to be part of it. I mean, I feel like a kid but who cares! I feel like a good kid.

'Of course, thank you. I just want to say I'm sorry and I hope Mr Gomez does order from us in the future.'

'I'll deal with Mr Gomez but in the meantime please check over your emails before hitting send,' he smiles again.

'Oh, one hundred percent. I won't be doing that again.'

'Well I hope not' He raises his eyebrows 'Kathy will send you an email with your list tomorrow morning,' he says and air quotes the word 'list'. 'Now it's quarter past five so we'd best be off. Go and have a good evening' and he signals towards the door.

As soon as I get out the door, I fling my head back a breathe a sigh of relief. Right, I need to get home and see Jack.

19.00

I have made a curry for us tonight because it's Jacks favourite and I'm trying to make up for being a drama queen. Also, it will go well with the Indian sweets he's bringing back. He seems to have forgotten the whole thing anyway but he did ask if he could be let off the list thing, which I suppose I can deal with.

20.00

Brad text me earlier today with a whole list of areas to research for the event from licenses and certificates to adverting platforms. There is so much to do! I am going to spend the evening making business plans. I was a bit reluctant at first because I am terrified at what the power of a list can do but then I remember that when you are in a car crash, the first thing people advise, is to get back behind the wheel so that's what I'm going to do.

I'm so grateful for how Brad takes my ideas seriously and helps me achieve what I set out to do. I start to text him because I know I have never actually told him that.

As I am typing, I think back to his reaction at lunch and laugh at how mad he thought I was. Then I think about the fight with Jack and I start to feel sad at how it could have ended. I really don't want the lists to have that affect. It's meant to be a happy thing.

Then it dawned on me. It's not about the list it's about the person writing the list. Each list that has been given to me has reflected the relationship I have with that person:

My Brother sent me a list in order to make me look stupid, but that's what little brothers do.

Kathy wrote a list to have power and control but she is my boss.

The groups of friends created lists for banter and to see how far I would go.

Josh used his to test me.

My Mum focused on my fears and dislikes to prove I am capable of anything.

My Nan wanted to seek the child within me she once knew and bring back memories.

Brad saw success in me and encouraged it.

And Jack didn't want to change anything about me, he chose me for a reason.

I sit there for hours pretending to watch TV but thinking about all the things I have done and how this has changed the way I think and live my life. I started this year wanting to be a Yes Man (Woman) but realised I have done it in my own way and will carry on List Life forever.

23.00

Brad are you free any weekends in May? I type.

Ermm, at the moment I'm free most weekends. I think I have a job on the 19th May though so best to avoid that one. Why?

Shall we do the event on the 27th May then?

Oh my God! Yes! Are we actually doing this?

We are actually doing this.

2020

Three years on and so much has changed since then. Some for the better and some for worse but all driven by one thing… List Life!

Firstly, I finally changed jobs, Brad insisted on adding 'Apply for a flipping job and stop moaning about it,' to my list and that night I applied for various jobs including yacht stewardess, yacht engineer and a property developer - specialising in…you guessed it, yachts. Turns out I need to live within a 20-mile radius of the sea to qualify for any of these jobs so I applied for another job in events. A week later I was called for an interview and I was successful. I now work in a music venue and only up the road so no more long morning drives on the motorway.

I would also like to mention that in the end it wasn't too bad. Kathy and I went for lunch the week after the meeting to iron out a few issues and we now get on really well but she left shortly after and was replaced by a cheeky lad from London who had some good banter to be fair (Don't tell him I said that). A few new girls started like Annie, Georgina, Maria and Queenie (nicknamed due to her ability to get men to anything she wanted and they would bow down to her as if being knighted). We are all now a really close-knit group of pals. I also found out that Bill's sister was in hospital at the time which explains why he was a bit stressed. He turned out to be a really nice guy. Plus, his sister is called Elise. Who would have thought it?

Monika and I go to salsa classes together every Wednesday with Louise and Graham. Natalie had to give it up because she had a little baby girl with her long-term boyfriend, Daniel. I was asked to be her God-mother but, as I have not been christened, I was asked to be a sponsor, so have to donate £2 a month (I'm joking, but I am her sponsor). When she was born, I knitted her a cute little cardigan and hat, assisted by Tom who used to give me lessons at lunch.

Big Nan sadly pass away from a short battle with cancer at the end of 2017, which left my Grandad campervanning on his own. However, we send each other lists on a regular basis which has resulted in me now playing drums. He put it on a list as a joke but rules are rules. I went for a free trial and loved it, so now I go every Monday and have played in a few pub gigs with the guys there. See it can lead you anywhere. Also turns out Nan was amazing at writing poetry and had written one about the lists. I have that poem framed on my wall at home.

Jack proposed last May and I said 'Yes!' Not because he put it on a list, in fact, to this day he has never written me a list. He says it's great and joins in with all the crazy things I get up to but he has never actually written one himself. I still wonder what he would put on it.

Last but not least…I officially own and run a mobile bar selling beers from around the world! The dream came true.

Brad and I researched the food idea for ages. We visited events most weekends in London and the local areas but decided to go straight in for the kill with the beer stall.

I went and got my personal license so that I am legal. We sat in a local pub for weeks, designing our marquee design, logo and advertising. We researched international beers and wrote to companies to see if we could sell at their events.

On the 13th June 2018, we drove up to Kettering to do our first event and it was amazing, such an achievement. I mean we hired a van, underpriced our beer and spent 3 hours lugging boxes of beer up and down the stairs of Brad's flat but never-the-less it was a success in our eyes. It was the first of many events that year. We attended music festivals, food markets, charity events, a local scarecrow competition, even a street wear promotion! It was fantastic! I mean, we made zero money in that first year but we learnt so much and it was worth it.

On the 14th May 2019 we received an email from a lady asking if we operated as a bar? We didn't have a bar at the time but decided to see if we could buy one. One night, while speaking with Brad's Dad, we designed a bar and he made it that weekend. We accepted the bar job and when the night came, we were so nervous. This was going to be make or break for us.

It started slow, because people were coming in dribs and drabs but by 9pm it was heaving. The night was manic. We sold more beer than we had for the previous year's events put together.

From that night on we have only ever done two more public events. We now operate as a mobile bar specialising in world beer. I love it!

List life has changed my life and has impacted other lives too. Just proves that letting go of control and putting trust in others can really highlight your ability to do anything. You just have to try.

Printed in Poland
by Amazon Fulfillment
Poland Sp. z o.o., Wrocław